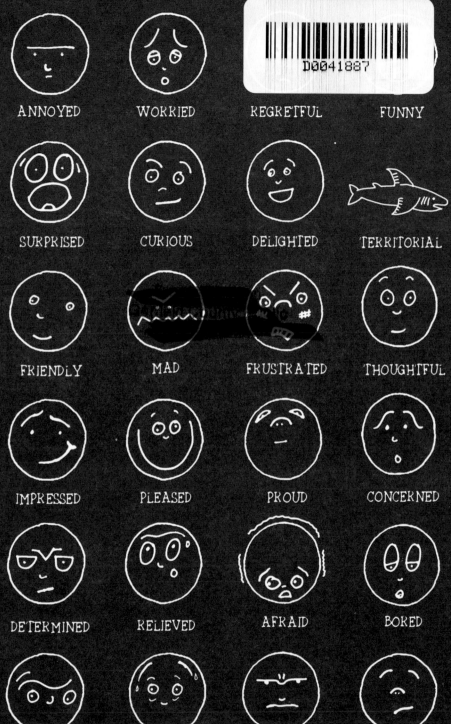

ANNOYED · WORRIED · REGRETFUL · FUNNY

SURPRISED · CURIOUS · DELIGHTED · TERRITORIAL

FRIENDLY · MAD · FRUSTRATED · THOUGHTFUL

IMPRESSED · PLEASED · PROUD · CONCERNED

DETERMINED · RELIEVED · AFRAID · BORED

UNDECIDED · NERVOUS · ANGRY · SMUG

COLIN FISCHER

COLIN FISCHER

ASHLEY EDWARD MILLER & ZACK STENTZ

razor
bill

An Imprint of Penguin Group (USA) Inc.

Colin Fischer

RAZORBILL

Published by the Penguin Group
Penguin Young Readers Group
345 Hudson Street, New York, New York 10014, U.S.A.
Penguin Group (USA) Inc., 375 Hudson Street, New York,
New York 10014, U.S.A.
Penguin Group (Canada), 90 Eglinton Avenue East, Suite 700, Toronto,
Ontario, Canada M4P 2Y3 (a division of Pearson Penguin Canada Inc.)
Penguin Books Ltd, 80 Strand, London WC2R 0RL, England
Penguin Ireland, 25 St Stephen's Green, Dublin 2, Ireland
(a division of Penguin Books Ltd)
Penguin Group (Australia), 250 Camberwell Road, Camberwell, Victoria 3124,
Australia (a division of Pearson Australia Group Pty Ltd)
Penguin Books India Pvt Ltd, 11 Community Centre,
Panchsheel Park, New Delhi – 110 017, India
Penguin Group (NZ), 67 Apollo Drive, Rosedale, Auckland 0632, New Zealand
(a division of Pearson New Zealand Ltd)
Penguin Books (South Africa) (Pty) Ltd, 24 Sturdee Avenue,
Rosebank, Johannesburg 2196, South Africa

Penguin Books Ltd, Registered Offices: 80 Strand,
London WC2R 0RL, England

10 9 8 7 6 5 4 3 2 1

Copyright © 2012 Ashley Edward Miller and Zack Stentz

ISBN 978-1-59514-578-9

Library of Congress Cataloging-in-Publication Data is available

Printed in the United States of America

ALWAYS LEARNING   PEARSON

FROM ZACK:

For Sophia and Dash, and all they've accomplished.

For Ian, always there to help and guide them.

For the real Mr. Turrentine, who accepted no excuses.

For my mom, a more effective therapist than even she realized.

And for Leah, who showed me that empathy comes from a place beyond understanding.

FROM ASHLEY:

For my mother, educator and creator of a book-eating, story-spitting monster.

For Caden, my monster-in-training.

And for Jennifer, who believes in monsters.

INTRODUCTION

Lev Grossman, bestselling author of *The Magicians*

For most people, crime scenes are places to avoid. You see that yellow police tape and all you can think is: thank God I'm on this side of it. You look, of course—everybody looks, though usually you don't see anything more interesting than a couple of men or women in blue with serious expressions on their faces, and maybe someone in plain clothes who looks like they're wishing they were on your side of the tape too. But then you keep on walking. You leave it behind, like a bad dream.

A crime scene is another world—it's a bit like Narnia. Past the yellow tape you become a new person: you're recast as a victim, a suspect, a witness, a detective. Things aren't things anymore, they're evidence, to be pieced together into a story according to the principles of forensic science and logical deduction. They're clues to the question on everybody's minds, which is: what the hell just happened here?

That's if you're you. Or me. If you're Colin Fischer, forensic science and logical deduction are the principles you use to get through everyday life. The scene of the crime is where he lives, all the time. For Colin the entire world—his home, his school, his neighborhood—is a mystery. And he is the detective.

He isn't really a detective, of course. Colin is fourteen years old. He's just starting his freshman year at West Valley High in the San Fernando Valley. It's not a situation where the techniques of criminal investigation would ordinarily apply. But Colin isn't an ordinary kid; he suffers from Asperger's syndrome. "It's a neurological condition, related to autism," he explains to his gym teacher, with characteristic precision. "I'm diagnosed as high functioning, but I still have poor social skills and sensory integration issues that give me serious deficits in areas of physical coordination."

He's not exaggerating—because Colin only ever says exactly what he means—but he might be slightly underdramatizing the issue. Colin is different. He doesn't like to be touched, even by his parents. He can't tolerate loud noises. He has a hard time reading facial expressions; he keeps notes on what faces correspond to what emotions, so he can match them up with the people around him and tell what they're feeling. He has an amazing memory and prodigious reasoning skills, and he's extraordinarily knowledgeable in certain areas—game theory, for example, and the history of the U.S. space program—but he also has trouble grasping things a five-year-old would know automatically, without trying. Watson once said about Sherlock Holmes, "His ignorance was as remarkable as his knowledge." You could say the same thing about Colin.

It won't surprise you to hear that Colin keeps a framed portrait of Sherlock Holmes over his bed.

Colin's high school experience isn't a typical one. This isn't a Judy Blume novel. You don't read *Colin Fischer* and think, "Yeah, I remember that time a cell phone rang in math class and I got so freaked out I had to bark like a dog 'til it stopped." Colin is more like an alien anthropologist stranded on Earth, with no choice but to master the local social codes and try to pass as human, or perish.

But that's what makes Colin's story so important, and so interesting. Because maybe we're not quite as human as we like to think we are, either. Maybe we're a bit weirder than we like to pretend. We like to believe that everything about our lives is neat and clear and unambiguous, but it isn't. Look at the faces of the people around you: how often do you really know what they're thinking and feeling? How often does something happen that you can't explain—a book that isn't where you left it, a question you should know the answer to but don't, a friend who walks by without saying hi? We like to believe our lives aren't bizarre, that we always know what to do or say, that we know what the hell is happening all the time. That our lives are in no way like a mystery.

But of course we don't always know what's going on. Life is confusing. We're constantly trying to piece together a coherent story out of the clues all around us, and the evidence doesn't always fit. In that sense, mysteries aren't unusual; they're not the exceptions, they're the rule. We're not all Sherlock Holmes, or Colin Fischer, but the difference is not one of kind, just one of degree. We're all on the same scale; they're just a couple of standard deviations out from us.

So what happens when a boy for whom everything is a mystery, for whom an ordinary classroom is a crime scene, comes across a real mystery? A real crime, with a real suspect and real evidence, and a real gun, right in the middle of his high school cafeteria?

Suddenly the tables are turned. Suddenly everybody around Colin is freaking out. They're out of their element—but Colin isn't. This is his element. He's been preparing for this role, the role of the detective, his whole life. We're in his world now, the world on the other side of the yellow tape, and for once in his life Colin is right at home. This is where he lives, this is his home planet, and it's the rest of us who are aliens here. "Life," Holmes once said, "is infinitely stranger than anything which the mind of man could invent." We like to forget that. Colin is here to remind us.

PART ONE:
BIRTHDAY CAKE AND A GUN

CHAPTER ONE:
SHARK BEHAVIOR

In the open ocean, fish often swim together in schools. This is typically a strategy to find food or evade predators. But in the waters off the Galápagos Islands there is a school of fish like no other in the world. . . .

Thousands of hammerhead sharks congregate and swim in intricate patterns, the only species of shark to exhibit schooling behavior. Scientists still don't know why.

Have they come here to feed and take refuge in a hostile ocean? Are they selecting potential mates? Or are they engaging in mysterious social behaviors that an outside observer could never understand?

My name is Colin Fischer. I'm fourteen years

old and weigh 121 lbs. Today is my first day of high school.

I have 1,365 days left until I'm finished.

Colin clutched his precious, dog-eared Notebook to his chest. The Notebook had seen better days, though it had been fastidiously cared for. Its red cover was faded, the metal spiral down its side showed the wear of a slow but inevitable unraveling, and the holes in the cardboard were worn down from constant opening and closing.

The Notebook, in Colin's way—unspoken, but demonstrated—was loved.

He pushed his way through the sea of humanity around him, sometimes bobbing, sometimes swimming, eyes downcast to avoid the gaze and attention of any predator that might hunt the hallway. Collisions with other students occurred, though infrequently, in spite of Colin's best efforts. "Excuse me," he would say without looking as someone brushed his arm. "Please don't touch me," as elbow met elbow. "I'm sorry."

Colin's eyes flicked upward, having counted every step before this last one, knowing there were precisely twenty-seven between his locker and the Boys' Room. The heavy wooden door dwarfed him, and for a moment Colin fixed on the blue triangular sign just next to it. Colin didn't like the color blue. It made him feel cold.

Still, he pushed against the door, taking care to

protect the Notebook from coming into contact with any part of it—especially the blue triangular sign.

The Boys' Room was dimly lit and dirty. Colin carefully set his Notebook on a narrow black shelf and stood at the white porcelain sink. He noted with a wince that the sink itself was not very clean or well-cared-for, and after a moment's hesitation turned on the faucet (one turn–*beat*–two turns–*beat*–three turns, now *wash*). Two drops of soap from the dispenser—blue, which Colin didn't like, but there was nothing to be done about it.

It was only after rinsing his hands, when his bespectacled eyes met his own in the decaying mirror, that Colin realized he was not alone. Wayne Connelly stood behind him.

Wayne was a beast, Colin's opposite in every way. He was broad, thick, giving the impression that he might have been carved out of solid rock rather than born from flesh-and-blood woman. Colin turned toward him, and Wayne smiled.

Colin scrutinized the smile. Analyzed it. What did it mean? He pictured a series of flash cards, each with a different sort of smile drawn on it, each carefully hand-labeled for proper identification:

FRIENDLY. NERVOUS. HAPPY. SURPRISED. SHY.
CRUEL.

"Hello, Wayne," Colin said, as if he were reading from a script. "How are you today?"

Wayne's smile widened as he grabbed Colin, quick for someone of his size. His indelicate fingers twisted the material of Colin's striped polo shirt, then hoisted him into the air and carried him toward a bathroom stall.

"My shirt," Colin observed. "You'll ruin it."

"Bill me, Fischer," Wayne answered. He kicked the stall door closed with a loud *clack* that made Colin shudder. "After you say hello to the sharks."

CRUEL, Colin decided as his head went into the toilet, thrashing but helpless. The smile was definitely CRUEL.

CHAPTER TWO:
THE PRISONER'S DILEMMA

I want to tell you about a problem.

It is called "The Prisoner's Dilemma," and it's very interesting because it is a math problem about telling the truth. The problem does not concern real prisoners, just hypothetical ones. "Hypothetical" means it is a logical construct, a scenario to help illustrate the problem space.

It goes like this: Two criminals collude on a robbery. They are arrested and taken for questioning by the authorities. The problem concerns how they answer, and the consequences of the information they choose to provide. The prisoners have two possible strategies to deal with the police: They can "cooperate" with each other, or they can "defect." "Cooperate" means they lie, and "defect" means they tell the truth.

> I think it would be simpler to say "lie" and "tell the truth," but I did not make up the problem.
>
> If both prisoners lie, they both get a minimal sentence. If one lies but the other tells the truth, the liar gets the maximum sentence and the honest one goes free. If both tell the truth, both receive a minimal sentence with early parole.
>
> This means it is better to tell the truth. A lie will never pay off, and it may cost you a lot.

The Fischer house was in every way ordinary.

Nestled in the northwestern corner of the San Fernando Valley, it more or less resembled every other house nestled in the northwestern corner of the San Fernando Valley: two stories, a beige exterior, and architecture that attempted (halfheartedly) to evoke Spanish colonialism.

The backyard contained one unique feature: a trampoline, well-used, bought for Colin when it was discovered that bouncing helped him relax, focus, and think. Here, reassured by intermittent weightlessness, he was free to imagine himself unbound by earthly concerns. Up-down, up-down, up-down . . . usually for hours, and always alone.

Colin stood at the gate, eyes fixed on the trampoline, his hair matted and his clothes soaked. In his hand, he clutched his Notebook, which had mercifully been spared Colin's unexpected and unwanted encounter with the toilet. For a moment, he considered losing himself to the trampoline's elastic embrace—but then he thought better of it. His wet clothes would in turn make the trampoline wet, and that simply would not do.

Instead, Colin hurried up the walk and burst into the kitchen.

He barely registered the presence of his parents and younger brother gathered around the breakfast table, so he did not see their looks of surprise and concern, or in Danny's case, the look of weariness, exasperation, and vague dread. Even if he had seen them, Colin would have had neither the time nor the inclination to process or understand them. Colin was on a very particular mission, on his own particular timetable.

Mrs. Fischer checked her watch: eight A.M. "That was a quick first day," his mother observed, her irony as lost on Colin as it usually was. "Taking 'homeroom' kinda literally, aren't we?"

Mr. Fischer nodded as he rose from his place at the table. He started after Colin like a border collie off to round up an errant sheep. "Whoa there, Big C."

Colin stopped in his tracks, a learned response to his father's kind but commanding voice. He turned toward his father, head tilted down, avoiding his gaze— not out of shame, but because Colin avoided any gaze unless absolutely necessary. It had the effect of making the boy seem perpetually sad, although he almost never was.

"Lose a fight with a fire hose?" Mr. Fischer asked, watching the water drip from Colin's soaked polo shirt onto the tile floor.

His mother didn't wait for the answer. She was already halfway up the stairs. Fourteen years of the unexpected had trained her to swing into action on a moment's notice, even in the absence of complete information or explanation. "I'll get a towel."

Danny shook his head as he realized Colin's predicament and what had likely brought him to it. "Holy crap," he said. Then he saw his father's reproachful look and turned back to his pancakes. "Yeah, yeah. 'Eat your breakfast, Danny.' I know."

His mother reappeared a moment later. Colin took the towel she offered, careful not to touch her, and began to run it through his hair.

"So we're waiting for the story," his father said. He leaned against the kitchen wall with his arms folded, fixed on Colin with his particular, patient CONCERN, letting the suggestion hang there. You couldn't push Colin to do or say anything, but if you made your expectations clear, he invariably gave you what he felt you needed—if not precisely what you asked for.

"I got wet," Colin said, as if that explained everything. Which in Colin's mind, it did. Then he turned and climbed the stairs toward his room.

"Way to crack the old whip," Danny said, and went back to his breakfast.

The first thing a visitor to the Fischer house would notice about Colin's bedroom was the portrait hanging over his bed. It was a framed, black-and-white photograph of Basil Rathbone in a deerstalker cap and a houndstooth cloak with a long, curved pipe perched on the edge of his bottom lip. His pose was thoughtful and distant, as though he were aware of the photographer but possessed of greater concerns. He was in this portrait not Basil Rathbone at all—he was Sherlock Holmes.[1]

The second thing a visitor would notice was Sherlock Holmes's company. Photos of *Star Trek*'s Mr. Spock, Commander Data, even Detective Grissom from *CSI* all hung in places of honor on the wall. Once, Colin's father had taken the picture of Spock to be autographed—and had to replace it after Colin declared the photo "ruined" by Leonard Nimoy's signature. Mr. Fischer learned from this that Colin's room was a shrine not to actors he admired, but to cool, clear-headed logic.

The third thing a visitor would notice was Colin's floor, littered with piles. Piles of books. Piles of

---

1 Basil Rathbone was hardly the first actor to portray Holmes, nor was he the only one to do so. In fact, the first stage performance of Holmes was by Charles Brookfield in 1893, who portrayed the renowned sleuth in a production of "Under the Clock." However, Rathbone was most widely associated with the part and, in Colin's mind, the definitive inhabitant of the role of World's Greatest Detective.

magazines. Piles of toys and half-disassembled household appliances. The piles were everywhere.

To the untrained eye this was just a mess, not so different from the mess any other boy could have created in any other room in any other house. But its true nature was in its details—not as it appeared, as Colin might point out, but as it was. Neatly organized, like-with-like. There was a principle behind every pile in the room, even if understood only by Colin himself. For example, a magnetron from an old microwave sat atop a book about marsupials and several back issues of *The New England Journal of Medicine*, an organizational feat that defied even his parents' efforts to divine a connection.

Colin stood amid the piles in front of his desk, dripping wet, the towel draped around his shoulders. His gaze was fixed on a piece of paper filled with columns of crude, hand-drawn faces, each labeled with a word describing an emotion. The paper in turn was but one of many in a stack, a rough guide to understanding social intentions of the human animal. At the moment, Colin studied every imaginable species of the smile.

He looked up at the sound of sneakers on his hardwood floor. From the peculiar squeak and the weight of the step, he knew who had entered. "Hello, Danny," he said. "How are you today?"

Colin was only three years old when Danny was born. Like most children, he was fascinated by the prospect of a little brother or sister. Unlike most children, he expressed this by forcing his father to read him every page of *What to Expect When You're Expecting*. He asked pointed questions of his mother, her eating habits and general health. He was present for the sonogram when the new baby's sex was determined. He was unusually involved in every aspect of the pregnancy and cried when he was informed he would not be welcome in the delivery room. Colin seldom let his baby brother out of his sight. He recorded his observations in drawings and, on the eve of Danny's first birthday, presented a complete dossier entitled "Things We Know about Danny" to his parents. In fact, the first entry in Colin's first Notebook was about him:

> I have a brother. His name is Danny. He likes to smile. My mother says he is happy because he has a big brother who loves him.
> Investigate.

Danny didn't answer Colin's question. He knew it was just part of Colin's social script and made no secret of his hatred for the forced, almost robotic nature of Colin's interactions with him. "So," Danny began, "somebody took your head on a grand tour of the boys' bathroom. You know, the full Tidy Bowl treatment. Am I right?"

"My behaviorist Marie says, 'Kids are often

frightened of anyone different. They make themselves feel secure by picking on kids who are.'" This was repeated word-for-word, precisely as Marie had said it to him.

"You're not different," Danny said with a snort. "You're a carnival sideshow."

From outside came the sound of a diesel engine slowing to a halt and a soft, hydraulic hiss. Mrs. Fischer's voice rang up from down the stairs. "Danny, your bus! I am NOT driving you to school, compadre, so saddle up!"

Colin watched carefully as his eleven-year-old brother's expression visibly changed. "Just stop, Colin," Danny pleaded quietly. "Can't you just stop?" With that, he pounded back downstairs. Colin impassively turned his attention back to his guide. He flipped through the pages, trying to match a drawing to Danny's face.

Finally, he paused and placed his finger on a frown. "AFRAID."

Colin and his father rode in silence.

Colin wore fresh jeans and a simple burgundy T-shirt. Mr. Fischer was dressed for work, a blue button-down oxford with a twenty-dollar cotton tie and a pair of khakis, all neatly pressed. A Jet Propulsion Lab security badge was clipped to his shirt pocket, identifying him as "Michael Fischer, Senior Analyst." In the picture, he was smiling and *HAPPY*. Colin liked to look at the badge; his father's smile was comforting.

At the moment, Mr. Fischer was not smiling. His lips were pursed gravely, his fingers tapping out a slightly uneven rhythm on the steering wheel. Colin looked away from him. Instead, he stared out the window, considering the cars waiting at the 118 on-ramp. They had been merging in a neat left-right-left weave, an example of spontaneous self-organization. Then a woman in an SUV with a phone to her ear broke the pattern and threw it all into self-interested chaos. Colin found it very interesting how one small violation of the social order could throw an entire system out of balance.

"So," his father finally said, tired of the silence and convinced he couldn't wait Colin out on this one, "are you gonna tell me what happened? Or do I have to guess?"

Silence. Then: "You have an important meeting," Colin said. It was not an answer.

"It's the first day of school." His father pressed. He would not allow his son any opportunity to change the subject, as he was the master of it. "You couldn't have even made it to homeroom. Well, unless homeroom is in the swimming pool."

"Your shirt is pressed," Colin observed. "You never press your shirt unless you have a meeting, and only if it's important."

This was true. It was also irrelevant. "I know it's

scary. It was scary for me, and I was a jock. I could take care of myself."

"You're drumming your fingers. That means you have to meet with someone you don't usually have to talk to. And you have to answer their questions."

Mr. Fischer stopped drumming and glanced at his hands. When Colin was right, he was right . . . which was nearly all of the time, actually. "I'm sorry you're on your own in there now. I am. But that's how the system works."

Colin looked at his father finally. He understood everything. "The director," he said. "You have a program review. Is it the budget again?"

"It's too bad changing the subject isn't a business. You'd make a killing." He turned the car into the West Valley High School parking lot. "I'm not gonna make you talk to me," he said. "I just want you to know you can."

"I am talking to you."

His father sighed, defeated. He held up a hand and splayed the fingers apart.

"Coming in for a landing." This was a warning, letting Colin know he was about to be touched. Colin didn't like to be touched by anyone, even his parents, although he was tolerant if given proper notice. On some level, he understood their need for contact. He had read about it in a book.

Colin braced himself as his father reached out and

touched his shoulder. A gentle squeeze. "Have a good day at school."

Colin nodded silently and got out of the car. Mr. Fischer watched him trudge up the walk, head down and body hunched. He felt a pang of worry, then helplessness,[2] a recognition on his part that no matter what, eight hours a day for the next four years, Colin would be alone.

The hallways were packed with students, teachers, and staff, all pushing past each other in transit as the first bell rang.

Colin winced a little at the sound—too high, too shrill, and too staccato. The first time Colin heard a school bell had been three years earlier. He had shrieked with terror at the unexpected cacophony and continued to shriek until the bell finally stopped ringing. In time, and with a great deal of effort, he learned to control his response to the noise. It was now anticipated, its effects dispelled through slow, silent counting.

---

2 Despite being a concept of seemingly ancient origin, the word *empathy* was only coined in 1909, an attempt by an English author to find a scientific Greek word to describe the German term *Einfühlung* ("to feel into"). Psychological researchers later divided the term into many different subcategories of empathy. The kind manifested by Mr. Fischer as a physical reaction to the distress of another person was called *affective empathy* and was completely alien to his son. Colin did, however, experience *cognitive empathy*, which was an understanding of another's suffering reached through intellect instead of emotion.

On the mental count of "three," the bell stopped. Colin took a deep breath . . . then held it as he heard a familiar sound from around the corner, one that was almost as worrisome as the school bell: the voice of Wayne Connelly.

"Eddie's head, meet wall." Something heavy collided with concrete, a soft *crack* like the sound a melon makes when dropped on the sidewalk, only more violent. Colin crept around the corner, his curiosity getting the better of him. He flipped opened his Notebook and produced a green ballpoint pen to record what he saw:

> Wayne Connelly in fight with Eddie Martin. Shoving. Eddie wears a football jersey over a white T-shirt, blue jeans with high-top shoes. Other boys in football jerseys watch fight—Stan and Cooper. Stan has prominent gap in front teeth. Cooper exhibits pronounced ectomorphism. They are both tall. (All on football team? Cooper's frame lacks the standard muscle mass associated with the sport. Kicker? <u>Investigate</u>.) They do not help.

Eddie was up against the wall. He tried to shove Wayne back, but nothing happened. Then he swallowed hard, more than a little afraid. Eddie's friends, Stan (prominent gap in front teeth) and Cooper (exhibiting pronounced ectomorphism), looked at each other, nodded, and stepped forward to help.

Wayne turned on them with a snarl. "Back off," he growled. "I've got one foot for each ass."

Colin raised an eyebrow and counted. Three boys. Two feet. Curious.

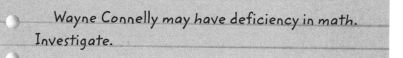

Wayne Connelly may have deficiency in math. Investigate.

Stan and Cooper didn't seem to care if Wayne could count. They understood his meaning well enough, frozen in place as Wayne stared them down. Finally, Wayne gave Eddie another quick shove into the wall and let him go. He stormed away.

Eddie glanced around the hallway, the focus of stares from everyone in the hallway. He collected himself. "Yeah—keep walking, wimp!" he called as he stripped off a blue-and-gold Notre Dame basketball jacket and hurled it into his locker. Wayne did not look back.

A girl, Sandy Ryan, emerged from the crowd and wrapped her arms around Eddie in a hug, pushing past Stan and Cooper. Eddie's friends made way for her. Cooper sighed with thinly veiled *EXASPERATION*, but Stan's eyes drifted down the back of her body with a half smile that Colin couldn't quite place. Eddie apparently had no such difficulty—he narrowed his eyes at

Stan with a TERRITORIAL frown, an expression so primal that Colin would have understood it as a toddler even if he had no name for it.

> Sandy Ryan in romantic relationship with Eddie.
> Likely consequence of breast development and
> prominence of secondary sexual characteristics.
> Investigate.

Sandy was blonde with skinny legs like a chicken—a physical attribute Colin had associated with her since preschool—but she was agreeably attractive in her freshman cheerleader uniform. "Eddie," she said in a low voice that seemed to have some visible effect on Eddie's breathing, making it slower and more regular. "It's not worth it. Wayne Connelly is a loser."

Colin poised his pen over his Notebook to record the moment, wondering idly if this made Eddie a "winner" by implication and if so what Eddie had won. Colin was so focused on his task, he was completely unprepared when Stan charged over to body-slam him into a locker. Colin was keenly and suddenly aware of his teeth clacking together, the constriction of his frame, and the slight give of the metal door as his body crashed into it. More than anything, and most distressingly, he could smell Stan's sweaty clothes— stale, at least a few days removed from an encounter with a washing machine.

As he collided with the locker, Colin's precious Notebook and green ballpoint pen tumbled from his fingers. His glasses were knocked from their perch and hung perilously from one ear and the tip of his smallish nose.

"If you're so worried about your little boyfriend, maybe you should go after him," Stan hissed through that gap in his front teeth. "Freak."

Colin adjusted his glasses. He felt a fire in his belly. In his chest. In his throat. He tensed his body, fighting back the blaze. If it continued to burn, Colin knew he would not be able to control it. It would get out. As Colin drew in a deep, cooling breath—

"Hey, Stan," a girl's voice said. It was gentle and clear. Pleasant. Colin liked the sound of this voice. It soothed him. The voice belonged to Melissa Greer.

In Colin's mind, Melissa was a skinny girl with a tangled mop of mousy hair, her face dotted with angry spots of acne, her smile caged by mirthless metal braces. Colin had noted over the years how other children would shun her, targeting her with their collective cruelty. During recess or after lunch, Colin would find Melissa alone in a corner of the playground, her face red and her eyes wet. He would not speak to her. He did not ask her why she looked SAD. He would simply sit on the ground next to her, knees huddled into his chest, and think of how cool the grass felt beneath him.

Of Melissa, Colin had once written in his Notebook:

Melissa Greer: Well-read. Good at math. Very interesting.

Melissa had changed over the summer. Colin noted her braces were gone. Her acne had disappeared. Her hair seemed tame. There were other changes Colin found very interesting. Stan, Cooper, and Eddie stared at her, noting many of the same things. None of them were quite sure what to make of this transformation.

"Holy crap." Stan blinked. He looked her up and down.

Melissa was not looking for anyone's approval, and she was long past crying on the playground. She nodded toward Colin, then fearlessly stepped into Stan's personal space with a smile—a rare event, and worth noting. Colin absently wished for his cheat sheet or a camera because this particular species of smile defied quick categorization.

"Go sublimate your homoerotic fantasies somewhere else," she said.

Stan looked at her blankly. "My—my what?"

Colin straightened his glasses. "She means you're confused about your sexual identity," he offered helpfully, "and you beat people up because you're secretly gay."

Stan scowled at Colin. Before he could say anything, Eddie gripped his shoulder. He seemed tired, as if the fight had aged him. "Stan," he said, "weight room in five."

Stan nodded slowly and backed off a little. He leered at Melissa. "You got hot. Call me." With that, Eddie, Stan, and Cooper disappeared down the hall with Sandy in tow.

"I missed you this summer," Melissa said as Colin leaned over to collect his Notebook and his pen. He dusted it off carefully, then pulled a worn cheat sheet from a pocket. The ink had faded to a spotty dark gray, the paper thinning at the creases from being folded, unfolded, and folded up again over seven years of almost constant use. Colin paged through it, looking back and forth between the pictograms and Melissa, comparing them. Finally, he found a match. In Colin's mind, he wrote the word *PLEASED* out over her head. "I can't believe you're in the halls without your shadow."

"Marie would just be a distraction here," Colin said. "I don't need a shadow."

A "shadow" was a person whose job was to follow Colin around and help him deal with the unexpected, the dangerous, or the potentially upsetting. Colin's shadow had been a woman named Marie. Colin liked her very much, although she often had to scold him for staring at her chest. Now that he was in high school, Marie had moved on.

Melissa nodded, agreeing but uncertain if Colin was correct.

"Your breasts got bigger," Colin announced. Melissa's cheeks ran red, and she laughed a little coughing laugh. She was used to Colin, but never quite prepared for him. Colin looked back at his cheat sheet. "*Embarrassed*," he observed aloud, erasing PLEASED and writing EMBARRASSED over her head. "Don't be. Breast development is a perfectly normal reaction to elevated hormone levels during puberty. Interestingly, it doesn't proceed at a uniform rate. . . ."

"Colin."

"It can be accelerated by a number of environmental factors, so it's not just genetics. For example, if your mother—"

"Colin," Melissa interrupted. "Please. Stop speaking."

Colin did. He waited patiently, remembering, as Marie had often advised, that sometimes people wanted to engage him in a discussion and had interesting observations and interjections to make.

"I . . . I know all that stuff," she said.

"Oh."

"So," Melissa said. *So* was a filler word, the kind people inserted into a paused conversation while they played for time to think of something more relevant or germane to the situation at hand. Colin rarely used filler words.

"Yes," Colin replied.

Melissa grabbed the Notebook from Colin's hand.

She whipped out a pen and started writing on the first blank page she found. Colin watched in horror but did not move to prevent this.

"If you need anything—anything—just call my cell," she explained. "Okay?"

She handed the Notebook back to Colin. He stared in disbelief at the ten-digit number Melissa had scrawled inside of it. "You wrote in my Notebook," Colin said.

Melissa smiled. The bell rang again. Colin counted to three. "See you," Melissa said. She scurried off to class as the halls emptied out, leaving Colin alone and holding his Notebook open to the page with Melissa's phone number. Fixed on it.

Colin sighed. "She ruined it."

CHAPTER THREE:
DETERRENCE

There is one thing I didn't tell you about the Prisoner's Dilemma, and that is that it's a problem in game theory, which is the study of competitive decision-making.

The Prisoner's Dilemma is a "non-zero-sum" game. This means all participants can benefit equally if they choose the right strategy. It was invented in 1950 by two mathematicians working for the RAND Corporation, which is a government think tank. However, the mathematicians were not interested in the behavior of prisoners. They were interested in war—specifically, nuclear war and how to prevent it.

What is interesting is that the Prisoner's Dilemma is a paradox. Cooperation only benefits an individual player when both players cooperate.

Otherwise, cooperation is punished. The paradox is easy to resolve if both players know what the other will do because most will take a small gain over a large cost.

But that's not how the game works. You can never know what the other player is going to do, so you have to rely on him to choose wisely. This is called "deterrence." It means that you are less likely to choose a risky strategy with a large negative return because you know your opponent has a compatible goal: survival.

The alternative has a name too. It is called "mutually assured destruction."

Of all the subjects in school, math was Colin's favorite.

Unlike most of his peers, Colin knew what math was for. He understood why it was useful to calculate the time two trains pass if one leaves Chicago at three P.M. headed east and another leaves New York at four P.M. headed west. The answer to the word problem was immaterial, but the *calculation* was of critical importance because it allowed one to learn about trains. Trains were very interesting to Colin and worth learning about.[3]

---

3 The problem is an illustration of fundamental principles of algebra. To determine the time X, one needs to plug in values for distance and speed, then resolve for both sides of the equation. What matters is not when each train leaves the station, but the distance between the two trains at the start of the problem and the end of the problem. Finding the

For Colin, this was true of all subjects. To learn a thing was to know a thing; to know a thing was to understand a thing; to understand a thing was to face it without fear.

So it was with great interest that he transcribed every word uttered or scratched on the board by his grizzled old algebra teacher, Mr. Gates. For example, the words "Identity Matrix." Gates's crooked index finger, dusty with chalk, pointed out at the class.

"Can anyone list the properties of an identity matrix?" Mr. Gates asked.

Colin could. His hand shot upward, expecting to be called upon. He was not. Mr. Gates silently noted Colin's clear enthusiasm and passed him by. "Thank you, Mr. Fischer," he said. "I'd like to see what other people know."

Low laughter rippled through the class. The loudest laughs came from the back and a boy named Rudy Moore—*Rudolph Talbott Moore* on Mr. Gates's student list.

Colin found Rudy troubling. His expression never matched the hand-drawn figures on his cheat sheet. Rudy's eyes and mouth always seemed to

---

solution is a simple matter of calculating the moment when the distance covered by each train relative to its speed is exactly equal. Colin once illustrated this to his parents by placing two electric trains on a track and predicting the exact moment he would crash them together. His father was impressed with Colin's math, but less so by the damage to his favorite trains.

disagree—in fact, his eyes almost never changed. It was as if he didn't really feel anything and simply moved his facial muscles to approximate human emotion. Rudy reminded Colin of a shark, especially when he smiled.

Colin had made precisely one personal observation about Rudy in his Notebook:

Rudy Moore: Intelligent. Dangerous. Avoid.

Mr. Gates made a low noise, almost a growl. "Anyone?"

Colin thrust his hand into the air again, interpreting the question as an invitation.

"Come on, someone give it a shot."

Colin waved, flagging his teacher down, thinking perhaps he didn't see him.

Mr. Gates froze, as if taking a moment to process some arcane algorithm before announcing his solution. "Okay. Fischer."

Colin stood and opened his mouth to speak. Before the first word of his answer could escape, he was interrupted by the shrill sound of a cell phone ringing from somewhere in the back of the classroom. Colin pursed his lips, silently counting to three.

Mr. Gates glared. "Whoever that is, turn off the phone or it belongs to me."

The ringing stopped. Mr. Gates held a moment just

to make sure it was really done, then nodded at Colin. "Go ahead."

Once more, Colin opened his mouth. This time, the cell phone interrupted him with a song: "The 1812 Overture." Once more, he counted to three, taking deep breaths.

"Knock it off," Mr. Gates snapped. "Last warning."

The music ended. Colin heard laughter and whispered conversation all around him and found it distracting. Frustrating. His heart pounded in his chest, cold sweat beaded on his forehead. The fire inside had rekindled, and it was building.

Colin forced the words out between breaths. "An identity matrix is—"

A cacophony of sound drowned out the rest of his words. The cell phone again. Loud and shrill. Not stopping. Not music, not a ring, not anything pleasant— just noise.

Colin put his hands to his ears to shut it out, only dimly aware of Mr. Gates charging down the aisle. He squeezed his eyes shut, gasping as the rest of the class laughed and pointed, and Mr. Gates searched in vain for the source. This was all too much for Colin to bear, so he did the one thing he knew would drown out the noise.

Colin barked like a dog. Louder and louder, so focused on his barking he didn't notice Mr. Gates discover and shut off the offending phone. He didn't notice the stares in his direction from around the room. He didn't notice

Rudy Moore's mouth open wide in deep laughter, show-ing off his shark teeth with his dead eyes.

Most of all, he didn't notice himself collapse to the floor, huddled in a ball with his hands over his ears, still barking as Mr. Gates called the school office for help.

This was the second time Colin had visited Dr. Doran, the school principal.

The first was three weeks before school began. He had come with his parents to discuss his special requirements, especially now that he would be without Marie. Dr. Doran was new to West Valley High School and brought with her new ideas about how to do things. She seemed interested in Colin's case and was firm in her reassurances that her approach to "mainstream-ing" would put his needs first and the convenience of the faculty second.

During the meeting, Colin's mother did most of the talking, his father asked most of the questions, and Colin spoke not at all. Instead, Colin spent the hour studying Dr. Doran's office, subjecting everything he saw to careful scrutiny.

In his Notebook, Colin wrote:

> *Dr. Doran's office: Clean, well-organized. Books on education and child psychology. Post-it notes stick out from some of the pages. Other books*

> on management and organizational politics also
> in evidence—paperback, dog-eared. She likes
> to read. On her desk, pictures of Dr. Doran with
> her family. One shows her smiling with a man and
> young boy, perhaps three years old—husband
> and child? This appears to be from ten years ago,
> although there are no further pictures of the boy.
> More recent photos show only Dr. Doran and the
> man. She does not smile in them.

Colin spoke only nine words to Dr. Doran, and he saved them for the end of the meeting. "Dr. Doran," Colin had said then, "I am very sorry for your loss."

Once again, Colin found himself doing very little talking in Dr. Doran's presence. She was staring at him over steepled fingers, sitting back in her chair. The cell phone Mr. Gates had found was on the desk before her. Colin looked at his feet.

"I know it wasn't your fault," Dr. Doran said evenly. "But I do hold you responsible for how you choose to react to things that upset you. Do you understand?"

Colin nodded. He offered no explanation because there was none.

"If and when something like this happens in the future, ask your teacher to excuse you from the classroom. You can come here, if you like, until you feel better."

Colin looked up at her. "What if my teacher says 'no'?"

"Your teacher will not say 'no.'" She meant it. Colin could tell. He trusted her.

"Let me be clear," she continued. "If there is another incident, I'll deal with you the same way I would deal with any other student here. Do you understand?"

Colin nodded again.

"You may go."

Colin stood, slung his backpack over his shoulder, and turned to leave. As he reached the door, he stopped and turned back toward Dr. Doran.

"Yes?"

He pointed at the cell phone. "Do you know whom that belongs to?"

"Not yet. But I expect we'll find out soon enough."

Colin shook his head. "No," he disagreed, "you won't. May I see it?"

Dr. Doran wrinkled her nose, then held up the phone so Colin could take it. He scrolled through the received calls. "You see?" he offered. "This telephone has only received two calls, both from a restricted number."

She rose to get a better look. Colin paged through the options on the phone. "No missed calls, no sent calls. There are no stored contacts, and no information on the owner other than the assigned area code and number. Don't you find that strange?"

"It's a new phone," Dr. Doran observed.

"Yes," Colin agreed.

He pulled a plastic sheet off of the LCD screen. "So new the owner didn't bother to completely unpack it. However, that is not what is strange about this telephone." He turned it over and ran his finger across the back. "Look at these scratch marks. They could only come from someone replacing a SIM card."

Colin reached into his backpack and produced a small screwdriver from a pocket toolkit (a curious investigator's best friend). He used it to pry open the back of the phone. Dr. Doran leaned forward to get a better look at Colin's impromptu forensic analysis. In spite of herself, she found this fascinating.

A narrow cover popped free, and Colin extracted its SIM card. "This SIM card came from a pre-pay telephone, making the owner completely untraceable."

"So where's the original SIM card?"

"With the person who bought this phone."

"And you're saying we can't figure out who that was."

"No, I'm saying you can't figure out who owned this phone just by looking at it."

Dr. Doran drummed her fingers against her desk and cocked her head slightly. Colin was going somewhere—it was a game he was playing, but she was pleased to play along. At least for the moment.

"It costs three hundred dollars," he continued. "I know this because my mother wanted to buy me one, and my father told her absolutely not would he pay that much money for something he was certain I would lose. Whoever bought this phone could afford to lose three hundred dollars. He also had the technical know-how to replace the SIM card and the forethought to plant the phone where Mr. Gates would not be able to find it quickly. Our adversary is intelligent, resourceful, and cunning."

"Our *adversary*," Dr. Doran repeated, a little dubious.

"Yes," Colin insisted. "This was intended for me. A ringing cell phone is a distraction in any classroom, but not worth three hundred dollars by itself. The person who did this knows me, and he knew how I would react. So whoever it was went to the same middle school I did and has taken classes with me in the past. That narrows down our list of suspects considerably." He returned the SIM card to its slot and handed the phone back to Dr. Doran.

"Okay, cut to the chase," Dr. Doran pressed. "Who was it? I'll suspend him so fast he'll think he's still on summer vacation."

"You'll never make it stick." Colin frowned. "Our adversary is too smart."

"Colin," Dr. Doran said, "just give me the name."

"Rudolph Talbott Moore," Colin said simply.

"And do you know why Rudy Moore would spend all of this money and go to all of this trouble just to make you bark like a dog? For a laugh?"

Colin shook his head. Adjusted his glasses. "The

choice of ring tones was a message, directed at me. 'The 1812 Overture.' It was a declaration of war."

"Yes, Colin. But why?"

"I suspect it has something to do with the Strange Case of the Talking Doll."

"What was strange about the talking doll?"

"It barked. Like a dog."

"I see."

"May I be excused?"

Dr. Doran nodded, and Colin exited without another word between them.

Colin was on the thirty-ninth step between the main office and class when he saw Sandy Ryan at Eddie Martin's locker. She had just finished popping open the door and was reaching inside to grab Eddie's Notre Dame jacket, which she slipped over her shoulders. Colin furrowed his brow and reached for his Notebook—was he witnessing a crime in progress? Could Sandy be so foolish as to believe she could get away with it?

> 10:15 A.M. Sandy Ryan at Eddie's locker. Is she a thief, or has her relationship with Eddie progressed to proto-cohabitation and a de facto communal property agreement?

If Sandy was aware of Colin, she gave no indication.

She just stood at Eddie's locker, frozen, evidently lost in thought. Colin crept closer, as though he were bird-watching and Sandy was a particularly skittish sparrow. He was about to record his further thoughts and observations on teenage relationship dynamics when he heard the school doors open and the *thud* of familiar, heavy footsteps. Wayne Connelly.

Wayne approached, silhouetted by the midday sun through the wide front doors. Colin noted the cool air blowing up the hall and realized the door behind Wayne was not quite closed. He was coming in from outside. Colin looked back to his Notebook. Sandy was forgotten. He barely registered the metallic *clank* of Eddie's locker slamming shut or the staccato *squish* of Sandy's tennis shoes against the tile as she hurried away. He frowned as he considered Wayne and noted the strangeness of the moment:

> Wayne, 3rd period. Comes in from outside. Very interesting. Investigate.

Wayne stopped, gaze fixed on Colin. Colin's eyes met Wayne's; he was surprised to see no MALICE on his usual tormentor's face, just HESITATION.

Colin closed his Notebook and put away his pen. He was on step number forty-three when he heard Wayne's voice.

"Where're you going?" Wayne asked.

Colin faced Wayne, reminding himself which step he was on so he would not lose count. "Hello, Wayne. I'm going to algebra. I'm missing a lecture on identity matrices, which I think are very interesting."

With a last look into the sunlit, open parking lot behind Wayne, Colin continued on his way. He hated to miss anything interesting—especially math.

CHAPTER FOUR:
THE KULESHOV EFFECT

My parents say it's hard to know what I'm thinking because most of the time I maintain a very blank expression. This is not something I try to do; it is just the way that I am. My father jokes that I "play my cards close to the vest," but this isn't true. It is just my face, whether or not I am playing cards, or any other competitive game.

As it turns out, however, the hardest facial expression for another human being to read is a perfectly blank face. This was demonstrated nearly a hundred years ago by a Russian director. After the 1917 Revolution, film stock was hard to come by in Moscow, so filmmakers would experiment with short pieces of scrap film. One director used his bits and pieces to demonstrate how editing could be used to manipulate human emotion.

First, he filmed an actor after instructing him to keep an absolutely neutral expression on his face. When the director followed the image of the actor with a shot of a roast chicken, audiences said, "Look how hungry that man is."

When he substituted a picture of a coffin, audiences thought the man was sad. If the image portrayed a beautiful woman, they said the actor was pining for his beloved.

This phenomenon is called "the Kuleshov Effect," after the director who conducted the experiments. What it demonstrated is that you can never tell what a blank face means until you know the context.

Colin smelled the inside of the gymnasium before he saw it. Stale human sweat, mildew, the faint aroma of urine from a leaky toilet in the boys' locker room, all unsuccessfully masked by an acrid, pine-based cleaning product. Colin tried to breathe through his mouth instead of his nostrils as he entered, but realized he could taste the cleaning solution on his tongue. An unfortunate consequence of the close relationship between the senses of taste and smell.

Colin focused instead on his sense of hearing as he padded across the empty gym. *Scrape. Scrape.* A tall, lean teacher hauled a massive net filled with basketballs across the hardwood floor.

"Mr. Turrentine?" Colin's voice echoed in the

gym's hard acoustics as the teacher looked up and met Colin's blue eyes with his own gray ones. Colin studied Mr. Turrentine's impressively bristly mustache. It reminded him of a silent movie cowboy villain or perhaps Soviet dictator Joseph Stalin.

"You're early," Mr. Turrentine said, "and you're scuffing my floors with those shoes." He pointed to Colin's black dress shoes, the laces double-knotted for safety. "We're not off to a good start."

Colin handed Mr. Turrentine a carefully folded slip of paper—a note from his parents. Colin was counting on it to exempt him from PE class. Mr. Turrentine scanned the note once, then twice, his face perfectly blank.

"Asperger's syndrome." Mr. Turrentine pronounced the words slowly but correctly. When most people said it, it came out sounding like "Ass-burger" (an endless source of amusement to Colin's younger brother and—until his mother put a stop to it—Danny's preferred nickname for Colin), but Mr. Turrentine was careful to make the "s" sound more like a buzzing "z," an artifact of the name's Austrian origin.

"What the hell is that?"

"It's a neurological condition related to autism," Colin explained patiently. "It was discovered by Austrian pediatrician Hans Asperger in Vienna in 1943, but not widely diagnosed until—"

"Autism," Mr. Turrentine interrupted. "You mean

like *Rain Man*?[4] You don't look like the Rain Man to me. Are you the Rain Man, Fischer?"

"I'm diagnosed as high functioning, but I still have poor social skills and sensory integration issues that give me serious deficits in areas of physical coordination."

Mr. Turrentine's mustache twitched slightly. Did he not like what he heard, or simply not understand it? Colin opted to explain it a little further. "That's why my parents and therapy team say I should be excused from this class."

Mr. Turrentine remained silent and impassive. It was as though the man had turned to stone. Finally, he spoke, his voice even and his words precise. "I can't accept this note."

Shock crept into Colin's usually even voice, causing it to go up a register. "But it clearly explains—"

"I know what it says, Fischer," Mr. Turrentine said. "I can read. And if I let everyone with two left feet skip out of my class, I'd be a very lonely guy. You don't want me to be lonely, do you, Fischer?"

"You're lonely?"

Mr. Turrentine's mustache twitched again. "I

---

4 *Rain Man* was a famous film from 1988, which featured Dustin Hoffman playing an institutionalized autistic man with savant-like counting skills and a variety of bizarre tics and mannerisms. It had won several Academy Awards, including Best Picture. Colin found this puzzling because as far as he was concerned the best movie of 1988 was *Die Hard*, starring Bruce Willis. Loud, but good.

assume you thought that little note of yours would do the trick, so you didn't bring gym clothes."

Colin nodded, impressed with his teacher's powers of deduction as he turned and moved briskly toward his cramped office at the far end of the gym. "Follow me," Mr. Turrentine said. "I'll see what I can find for you from the lost-and-found bin."

Colin froze. "These clothes don't have synthetic fibers, do they?"

"Only the best here at the house of Turrentine."

Colin wanted to feel relieved, but he suspected that Mr. Turrentine was making a joke—and at his expense to boot.

Twelve and a half minutes later, Colin marched onto the asphalt basketball courts of West Valley High, where the midday sun of the San Fernando Valley beat down on him with the relentless heat of the high desert. He had changed into his gym clothes alone in Mr. Turrentine's office, having rummaged through the discards for anything remotely clean and mostly cotton that might fit him. To Colin's dismay, even the best at the house of Turrentine assaulted his skin with petroleum-based fibers and his nostrils with the rancid, stale sweat of students long departed for college and the workplace.

Regardless of his current physical discomfort, Colin had a long-standing dislike of gym class and playgrounds. Putting aside the usual dangers of overly personal contact, the distasteful smells, and the unsettling, almost animal sounds of human play, Colin did not consider himself particularly coordinated. He could not throw; he could not catch. His only real physical gift, the only one that brought him joy (other than bouncing on his trampoline), was running. Colin loved to run. He learned to love it the first time he closed his eyes and felt the wind on his face, his body in motion, the sweat evaporating off his skin. Running made Colin feel alone and alive.

High school gym class seemed an altogether more threatening experience. Compared to Colin, many of the boys had sprouted into giants and seemed capable of crushing him without ever noticing he was there. For a moment, Colin hesitated. He took three deep breaths to prepare himself and continued gamely on.

The boys had formed into two lines, taking turns shooting free throws, each smoothly retrieving his ball and passing it to the next shooter before taking his place at the back of the line again. It was an infinite loop of dribbling, shooting, and jogging. The hollow, ringing *thud* of bouncing basketballs was punctuated by Mr. Turrentine's barked instructions that seemed to carry effortlessly over the din of directed play.

"Both feet behind the line, Ybarra."

"One smooth motion, McKee."

"Stop gossiping like old ladies and get to the back of the line."

Colin stepped across the court with robotic strides, clad in stained blue polyester sweatpants and a T-shirt emblazoned with a mouthless Japanese animated cat. As he approached, he heard familiar high-pitched laughter. It sounded like Stan, and indeed Eddie, Stan, and Cooper were waiting to shoot. Colin fixed his gaze on Eddie, trying to understand what the laughter was about, only vaguely aware it was directed at him.

Then he cast his eyes downward and focused on his breathing, trying to make each breath deep and even as he took his place with the rest of the boys.

Colin looked up as his turn came, just in time to see Eddie hurl the ball at his midsection. He batted it away rather than catch it, then, realizing his mistake, scrambled after the ball as it skittered toward an adjacent court.

"Fetch, Shortbus," Stan said, and laughed even harder.

"Shortbus" was a reference to the small yellow bus that trundled through the northwest corner of the San Fernando Valley, taking handicapped and developmentally disabled children from home to school and back again. Colin had never ridden it, but Eddie gave him the nickname in sixth grade. It had stuck to Colin ever since.

Pretending not to hear the giggles and mock cheers, Colin retrieved the ball and returned to his place in line. He dribbled it once, then tossed it overhand, sending it sailing over the backboard with at least a foot to spare. The schoolyard erupted in laughter at the spectacular miss. The noise was disagreeably loud, and now it came from all around. Mr. Turrentine whipped his head around at the sound of it and witnessed Colin lope gamely toward the baseball diamond after his lost ball.

His mustache twitched. "All right, keep it moving, people," he said to the three lines of basketball throwers. "Five more minutes, then laps, passing, and cool down."

For a moment, it was as if time had frozen. The laughter stopped, and so did the dribbling, the shooting, and the low buzz of conversation. Colin looked around at his classmates, wishing vaguely that he had his Notebook to record this unprecedented display of a teacher's power over his students. Then the silence broke, and a cacophony of dribbling, shooting, shuffling, and trash-talking resumed with renewed vigor. Colin realized that Mr. Turrentine was coming toward him with his quick but easy gait and took a moment to examine the man's feet—did they ever touch the floor?

"Fischer. Over here." Turrentine pointed to a vacant court. Colin approached it warily, cowering slightly as his teacher held a basketball in front of his face. The ball was close enough for him to observe the bumpy, fingerprint-like patterns on its surface. Colin wondered if he could calculate the total number of bumps from a one-inch sample and interpolating based on its total surface area, and so he did.

"Is this a live grenade, Fischer? Is it going to explode in your face?"

"No," replied Colin. Marie had spent several days over the summer trying to teach him to recognize a rhetorical question when asked, but he never got it right more than half the time. So he found it best to answer every question as if it had been sincerely asked. In this case, his answer seemed to meet with Mr. Turrentine's approval.

"You're a genius, Fischer. It is not a live grenade. It will not explode in your face. So don't throw it like you think it will."

Mr. Turrentine leaned in slightly for emphasis, looming. For the first time, Colin noticed a small constellation of raised moles on his teacher's right cheek. He tried to imagine how the man shaved around them without cutting himself, but left the thought experiment inconclusive as Mr. Turrentine snapped his fingers to regain Colin's full attention. "Step up to that line."

"Sir?"

"Did I misspeak, Fischer? Did I mumble, cough, or otherwise fail to articulate the fullness of my meaning? Step up to the line."

Colin appreciated the concreteness of the clarification. He obediently stepped up to the faded white line before him, then turned to face Mr. Turrentine.

"There is one and only one thing to understand about the game of basketball," Turrentine said. "God is a busy man. He doesn't have the time in His ineffable schedule to appear on my court and miracle your balls into a basket nine feet in the air."

"Mr. Turrentine?"

"Yes, Fischer?"

"I don't believe in God."

Colin waited for what he believed was the inevitable response. His lack of belief in a Supreme Being was longstanding, extrapolated from his third-grade deconstructions of Santa Claus and the Tooth Fairy, but he often encountered hostility when it came up in conversation.

Mr. Turrentine, however, remained impressively blank-faced. "Well, that's just fine, Fischer. Because I believe in you." He took a step to the side, observing Colin's stance. "Now, square your shoulders. Relax your elbows," he said. "Let them swing."

His words were crisp and clear. Not simply loud, but commanding. In fact, they weren't really *loud* at all—simply loud *enough*. Colin hypothesized Mr. Turrentine never shouted, though he allowed that future encounters could prove him wrong.

Mr. Turrentine reached to touch Colin's elbow to correct him. Instinctively, Colin drew back with a cringe.

"Please don't do that," Colin said in a small voice.

His teacher gave no indication of having heard him, but didn't try to touch Colin again. Instead, he demonstrated the free throw stance himself, letting Colin observe and then try to model the posture himself.

"Like this?" asked Colin. His positioning was an exact mirror of Turrentine's own. Eight years of occupational therapy had prepared him well to follow instructions on where and how to move.

"Just like that," Mr. Turrentine replied. Colin detected a new tone in his voice and tried to identify it. IMPRESSED, Colin decided. Perhaps AMUSED. He couldn't be entirely certain without a recording to review and further comparative study.

"Now, close your eyes." Mr. Turrentine waited a moment for Colin to comply. "Now visualize the basket, and the distance between your hands and the hoop. Then visualize throwing your ball into the basket. Are you seeing it?"

Colin stood with his brows furrowed and eyes darting rapidly back and forth beneath closed lids, almost as if he were dreaming. "No, I missed that one."

Mr. Turrentine watched Colin as he slowly dribbled the ball, his eyes closed, occasionally muttering phrases like "No" or "Not quite" and "Failure."

Colin wrinkled his face in consternation, wishing he had his Notebook to draw the picture first. But he didn't have his Notebook and doubted Mr. Turrentine would allow him to retrieve it. So he did the next best thing: He imagined he had his Notebook. In his Imaginary Notebook, Colin drew a schematic of the asphalt court, overlaid with a complicated force diagram depicting every variable involved in making or missing a shot. He included every conceivable factor, from the distance between himself and the hoop, to the estimated strength of the breeze he felt on his face. Satisfied that he understood the parameters of the problem, Colin extrapolated the diagram from his imaginary Notebook to a mental image of himself and the hoop in three-dimensional space. Colin threw shot after shot in his imagination, testing his calculations, finally arriving at the precise combination of angle, velocity, and spin that sent the ball careening into the basket.

"Got it," Colin said. His eyes snapped open.

He fired the shot without hesitation, launching the ball with both hands from directly in front of his chest. It traced a parabolic arc through the air and into the basket, making a slight whooshing sound as it passed through the net without touching the rim.

Colin blinked, not sure if he had really accomplished this or was going through another mental simulation. Other students who had been waiting for him to fail simply stood and stared.

"There, Fischer," Mr. Turrentine said. His expression was blank. "Like that. You're a damned basketball prodigy. Now retrieve your ball and get back in line."

Colin turned to chase after the basketball, then stopped as a thought occurred. He looked back at his teacher. "Mr. Turrentine," he asked, "are you God?"

"No, Fischer. I'm a gym teacher. I work for a living."

Satisfied by this answer, Colin trotted off after the ball, which had rolled to a stop at the half-court line. Colin picked it up, felt its weight in his hand, gauged the distance to the basket, and threw a one-armed shot. This, too, sailed cleanly into the basket, which Mr. Turrentine acknowledged with a nod and provoked a round of murmuring from the other students as Colin trotted past. Once was luck, twice was skill.

"Shortbus has a mean three-pointer," said Cooper, admiration leaking into his voice. Stan narrowed his eyes and glared as Colin took his place at the back of the line.

"Shut up," Stan said.

CHAPTER FIVE:
PRIMATE BEHAVIOR

People make many assertions about the uniqueness of human behavior that turn out not to be true. My fourth grade teacher, Mrs. Ferguson, once told our class that humans are the only animals to make and use tools. I tried to point out chimpanzees use narrow sticks to fish for termites, sea otters select rocks with which to open clams and abalone shells, and New Caledonian crows even bend wires into makeshift hooks. Mrs. Ferguson made me sit at the back of the room and didn't call on me for the rest of the school year.

What I find much more interesting than human uniqueness are the behaviors we share with our closest relatives: chimps, gorillas, and the other higher primates. For example, our response to danger. Most animals flee from the loud, the bright, and the unfamiliar; primates tend to move toward bright lights and loud noises, preferring to investigate and learn the cause of the commotion.

Humans and other primates are also the only animals to laugh when they are tickled—though I usually scream instead.

Colin sat alone at a table in the cafeteria, his back against the wall with a view of the windows and doors. This was what his father called "the gunfighter's seat." He called it this because he claimed that gunfighters in the Old West would always choose the spot in the saloon where they could best see danger coming.[5] Colin fully endorsed this as a policy but calculated the probability he might encounter an actual gunfighter anywhere to be exciting but vanishingly small.

Although the seat had been chosen for its view, Colin kept his head down. This allowed him to tune out the cacophony of clanging tableware, shouting, and conversation that might otherwise have overwhelmed him. He focused instead on cataloging the lunch his mother had packed for him: stick pretzels speared through slices of deli ham, baby carrots, celery sticks,

---

5 Colin attempted to verify his father's claim, although he never conclusively identified the origin of the term. To the best of his knowledge, it probably referred to Wild Bill Hickock, who famously preferred to sit in the most defensible position in any public location. Hickock himself demonstrated the wisdom of this policy when he accepted a seat in the middle of a saloon and was shot in the back for his indiscretion.

and a whole apple. Leaving the apple intact prevented oxidization and meant it would not turn brown over the course of the morning.

As he adjusted to the noise, Colin ventured to look up from his food and observe his peers. Over the summer, Colin's mother had rented a series of popular movies about high school from her teenage years, ostensibly to help him navigate this social minefield. He quickly lost interest in stories of gawky girls pining for popular rich boys and students from different cliques forming unlikely friendships while defying adult authority, leaving his mother to watch alone while muttering cryptic phrases like "I wanted a Blaine but ended up with a Duckie." However, it had given Colin enough data to formulate what he considered a working taxonomy of high school tribal groupings.

Colin watched his classmates with the detached interest of an anthropologist, recording in his Notebook the movements of the nerds, the popular girls, the jocks, the goths, the emo kids, and the most curious of all, the gangsta-wannabes. He scanned the cafeteria, and as his eyes flicked toward the double doors, he saw Melissa enter. Colin stopped writing.

Melissa was alone but smiling. She carried a worn red backpack, the same one she had carried all through middle school. Colin realized he wasn't the only one who had seen her—many people were looking her way. Especially the boys.

> 12:07 P.M. Melissa Greer enters cafeteria. Other students smile and wave at her. I do not recognize all of them from eighth grade, so they must be in her morning classes. Melissa smiles and waves back as she moves to a table in the middle of the cafeteria. It is under a banner that reads "WELCOME, STUDENTS." Melissa's friends Emma and Abby are there. There are party favors on the table. Today is Melissa's birthday.

Melissa beamed as Emma and Abby opened a brown grocery bag and presented her with a round white chocolate birthday cake, topped with white frosting accented by pink frosting roses. She clapped when she saw it, then looked up at her friends. As she did, she realized Colin was staring at her. Melissa smiled at him. WARM. Colin felt a sudden burning sensation course through his body. He looked away, developing a renewed interest in his carrot sticks as Melissa excused herself and headed toward him.

"Hello, Melissa, how are you today?" he said as she reached his table, trying to end each sentence on a slight up tone to convey enthusiasm and pleasure.

"I'm good," she said. Melissa's pale, freckled face reddened even more as the capillaries in her skin dilated and filled with blood. Colin recognized this as the "blush"[6] response—it was unique to the human

---

6 Blushing is the result of increased blood flow through the facial region, which has a higher concentration of capillaries and wider blood vessels

animal and still poorly understood by scientists. "I was wondering if you'd like to join us for some cake."

Colin studied Melissa's open, wide-eyed face. He attempted to identify her expression on his own for six seconds before he gave in and consulted his cheat sheet. Melissa appeared SHY. He pondered the meaning of this in silence.

"No," Colin said in a flat monotone. "I don't eat cake."

"Oh."

Melissa had known Colin long enough not to be surprised by his brusqueness. Still, the corners of her mouth turned down slightly and a thin furrow appeared along the length of her brow. EXASPERATED.

"It can't be because you're counting calories," she continued. "I'd kill to have your metabolism."

Colin raised an eyebrow. Curious. Melissa's body was lean and athletic. As far as he could tell, her metabolism was enviably speedy.

"It's not the sugar that's the problem; it's the texture. Cake is slimy and mushy, and I dislike foods that are mushy." Colin indicated the apple, pretzels, carrots, and celery arrayed in front of him. They were arranged

---

in the skin than elsewhere on the body. Some pseudo-scientific racists once argued that the ability to blush was a signifier of membership in the pure white race. This is not correct. It is a universal physiological response to emotion exhibited by all ethnic groups.

by color according to their position on the spectrum. "I enjoy crunchy foods."

"Uh, yeah," Melissa said. She pursed her lips. It was hard for Colin to decide what this meant. He pursed his own lips back at her, hoping this would invite a clue.

"Maybe next time I'll get you some peanut brittle." She smiled. FRIENDLY.

Colin perked up. "I like peanut brittle."

"Thought so," Melissa chirped, then turned to rejoin the impromptu party. As Colin tracked the graceful movement of her hips, he realized he rather enjoyed watching Melissa walk away. An unfamiliar, though not altogether unpleasant, flush of warmth bloomed through the skin of his cheeks.

To Colin's surprise, Melissa made a sudden detour toward a table occupied by Josh and Sundeep—two academically inclined boys toward whom she had been friendly in middle school. The boys were obviously of lower social status than the students at the table with the cake, yet Melissa took time to speak to them. "That is very interesting," Colin said to no one in particular, and opened his Notebook to record the moment.

The complexities of social groupings at West Valley High School were even more daunting than they had been at middle school, and Colin pondered strategies for untangling them. Perhaps, he thought, he could print out photos of the students from the school website and social networking sites, then pin them up on the cork board in his bedroom in a sort of social map—much like the ones the FBI used to understand the inner workings of drug syndicates and Mafia families. It would be very useful because over time he could add to the map and make changes as appropriate.

Colin began to sketch a very rough version of what such a social map might look like based on the people he saw in the cafeteria. He arranged the groups horizontally, with the vertical axis representing the person or group's relative position in the school's pecking order. The higher on the chart, the more popular that person was. Colin smiled at his solution. He prided himself on making charts that were intuitive and easy to read.

Colin started toward the bottom left of the page, writing Josh and Sundeep's names under the heading "Nerds."

In the "Jocks" column near the top of the page, Colin immediately wrote Stan and Eddie's names. He hesitated before adding Cooper, though, recalling that the tall, olive-skinned boy had a surprising talent for math. In fourth grade, Colin and Cooper shared a classroom, and Cooper consistently came in third or second in the room's weekly "math minute" contest. Colin, who won every week, had once attempted to compliment Cooper for his math skills, but the other boy had muttered, "Go away, spaz," and stopped speaking to Colin for the rest of the school year.

Emma the ace water polo player also went into the "Jocks" column. Beside it, Colin created a "Queen Bees" category to capture girls who seemed to have no talent or interests beyond the maintenance of their own popularity—a heading he took from the title of a bestselling book on the social anthropology of American high school girls. Abby went into that category. So did Sandy, with Colin drawing a line between her and Eddie to denote their intimate relationship (making a note to use color-coded yarn when constructing the board at home).

Melissa, Colin realized, would be a problem assigning to one group. As a cross- country runner and exceptionally intelligent student whose company was now seemingly in high demand, she had a foot in several different camps. Colin opted to table the Melissa question and moved on to Rudy Moore, whom he placed by himself at the top of the page.

Despite his presence in all the honors classes, Rudy was the only boy Colin knew who suffered none of the social demerits that accompanied extreme intelligence. Rudy had been popular for as long as Colin had known him. Colin wondered idly if there were some connection between Rudy's popularity and his penchant for cruelty. The ability to inspire fear was common among alpha members of any social species. Yet Melissa, too, was now popular, and she seemed to show as much kindness as ever.

Colin frowned and held the Notebook at a distance away from his face. Perhaps he wasn't designing this chart as well as he thought he had. As Colin pondered switching the X and Y axes or otherwise altering the chart, Emma and Abby suddenly thundered across the cafeteria, shrieking over each other in voices so high and so loud he cringed from the physical pain of listening to them.

"Melissa!" they shouted in unison. They looked at Josh and Sundeep the way a person might look at a friend's very ugly pet. "Wayne Connelly is eating your cake! You have to stop him!"

Melissa shrugged. She raised her brows, rolled her eyes, and finally allowed herself to be pulled back to the center table.

Colin turned his attention across the cafeteria toward Melissa. Wayne indeed stood at her table, grinning as he cut himself a huge slice of cake with a plastic knife. Her friends looked outraged, uselessly pounding Wayne with their fists, but Melissa just looked SAD. Colin rose from his seat, barely able to hear Melissa as she asked in a quiet voice, "What's your problem, Wayne?"

"No problem, Missy," said Wayne.

"*Melissa.*" They stood there a moment, staring at one another. There was an odd stillness Colin could not identify. "Whatever. Just take your cake. Take it and go."

Wayne didn't move. They kept staring. Colin felt his heart rate accelerate and his breathing grow rapid and shallow. Without knowing it, he'd balled his hands into fists. Colin marveled at his body's reaction as he realized something strange: He wanted to fight Wayne Connelly. This was odd because he had never wanted to fight anyone.

Before he could further analyze or act on this odd new impulse, Wayne finally broke eye contact and turned away from Melissa. "Where's the love, huh?"

Wayne sauntered away with his prize. He settled in at his own table, where he made a big production out of tucking into the piece of cake and carefully disassembling it layer by layer before eating it in surprisingly small, dainty bites. Colin watched, fascinated, the urge to do battle forgotten. Indeed, he found the incongruity of Wayne's fastidious eating so interesting he looked around the cafeteria to see how others ate.

Melissa darted at her piece like a hummingbird— small bites, methodically consumed. Rudy took a slice for himself but dumped it into the trash when he thought no one was looking at him. Sandy, still clad in Eddie's overly large Notre Dame jacket, folded a piece with a generous frosting rose into a large cloth napkin with the skill and delicacy of an origami artist, then gently deposited it into her large faux Juicy Couture handbag.

Colin's observations were interrupted by sudden movement across his peripheral vision, accompanied by rough male shouting. He whipped his head around, giving the impression of an owl spotting a mouse running across the undergrowth. His big eyes locked onto Stan, who—unwisely, Colin decided—clamped his hand down on Wayne's arm. He dug his thumb into Wayne's bicep, and Wayne winced in pain.

"This party doesn't accept food stamps," Stan said.

Colin puzzled for a moment: *Why would a party accept food stamps?* He abandoned this line of exploration as the fight escalated. Stan wrestled the piece of cake away from Wayne. Then Wayne regained his footing and shoved Stan into two of his friends, nearly toppling them. Colin flipped open his Notebook and uncapped his pen.

> Wayne Connelly has the strength of three high school freshmen. Diet and exercise? Investigate.

Despite his strength advantage, Wayne was still outnumbered. Stan and his friends advanced on the bigger boy.

"I am so gonna enjoy watching Eddie make you piss your pants," Stan said.

"Wow," Wayne said, his fierce expression unchanged. "I haven't been so scared since I saw your mom naked. Which would be . . . last night."

Colin understood that statement. Wayne was suggesting that he had had sex with Stan's mother, a vile insult and provocation across nearly every human culture and language. Stan responded with a snarl and shove, backed up by his friends.

Colin tensed. It looked as if a real high school fight was about to break out. Not a balletic exchange of punches, but a messy, chaotic rugby scrum. Thrown elbows, shoves, curses, and yelling. Lots of yelling. A crowd was gathering, encouraging the melee. Colin started to put his hands over his ears to shut it all out, just as Melissa's clear alto voice rose above the growing din. She was shouting. "All of you, just stop!"

"You're ruining everything!" Abby screamed. A split second later, one of the combatants—Colin couldn't see who—tripped into a chair and sent all four boys crashing into the table. Their tumbling bodies knocked over Melissa, Abby, Sandy, several other girls whose names Colin didn't know . . . and the cake.

If Colin had been a zebra, or a deer, or nearly any other mammal, he would have done the wise thing and moved away. However, Colin was a primate. Instead of moving wisely, he went for a better look.

Colin started forward just in time to see a flash of light accompanied by a loud, explosive *bang* that left his ears ringing.

The cafeteria filled with screams and shouts. Every student ran for the exits—every student except for

Colin, his fear of the noise overridden by his curiosity. He approached the scene of the fight, the smell of burned cordite and squashed mustard packets filling his nostrils. He looked down at the floor, noting smashed remains of half-eaten lunches, abandoned pencils and backpacks, a science-fiction novel, comic books, a tube of shiny melon lipstick and other make-up items, and . . .

A nine-millimeter handgun.

Its black metal barrel was still smoking slightly, rubber grip smeared with white chocolate and pink frosting. Colin's parents didn't keep firearms in the house, so this was the closest he had ever seen a gun outside a police officer's holster. Colin crouched down next to it, careful not to touch anything.

"This is very interesting," he said.

PART TWO:
THE FOOL AND THE FREAK

CHAPTER SIX:
EYEWITNESS INTERVIEWS

Modern forensic science is barely a century old, but the detective has existed far longer. Most scholars consider history's first detective story to be "Oedipus Tyrannus," by the Greek playwright Sophocles.

To end a plague, Oedipus must solve the murder of the previous king of Thebes. Oedipus's job would have been easier if he had had access to the tools of modern forensic science. Unfortunately, there were no DNA analyses or fingerprint databases in ancient Greece. I believe these would have been very useful, but they also would have made the play very short and far less interesting.

Without them, Oedipus was forced to rely on a tool that did not depend on technology: the eyewitness interview. He spoke to a Theban shepherd who had seen the old king killed in a roadside brawl. Through patient questioning, Oedipus discovered that same shepherd had many years earlier handed the king's infant son over to be raised by a stranger in Corinth. That infant grew up to be Oedipus.

This illustrates a key aspect of the eyewitness interview. Sometimes, you get answers to questions you never thought to ask. And sometimes, the answers make you wish you hadn't asked the questions in the first place.

Colin stepped into the nurse's office. It was decorated with antidrug posters, a picture of the USDA's food pyramid (which Colin noted was still ridiculously biased toward grains and dairy products), and colorful posters of the male and female reproductive systems. However, instead of the school nurse, two policemen stood in front of a cluttered desk. One was young, with a shaved head and a neatly trimmed moustache. He wore the dark blue uniform of the Los Angeles Police Department. The other man was a Latino in his thirties, wearing a leather jacket and baggy jeans. Colin knew he was with the police because an LAPD detective's shield hung on a lanyard around his neck.

"Are you Colin Fischer?" the detective asked.

"Yes," Colin answered. "Am I a suspect?"

The detective made a quick head-bobbing motion

Marie called a "double take." This typically denoted SURPRISE. "Now what would make you think you're a suspect?"

"It's only natural to suspect the person who was found standing closest to the gun," Colin said. "Also, I stayed in the cafeteria when the other students fled—this is an anomaly, and therefore very interesting. Combined with developmental issues the school safety officer will no doubt be familiar with"—he indicated the uniformed officer, who was indeed holding a folder marked **FISCHER, C.**—"all of this makes me an obvious choice."

The detective looked at Colin in silence for several seconds, scratching his neck. Colin noticed a faint trace of blue ink where he scratched, a faded spiderweb tattoo pattern that had been removed by laser at some point in the past. "You're not a suspect, Colin," the detective finally said, "but since you were very close to the gun when it went off, you're a potentially valuable witness."

"I understand," Colin replied.

The safety officer looked down at a sheet of paper. "You told the assistant principal that you didn't see who had the gun before it went off," he said, reading ahead. His lips moved slightly. "Is there anything you didn't tell him?"

"No, I was very thorough."

"Because it's safe to tell us if you did," the detective added. "So. If there's anything you want to add . . ."

"Yes," Colin declared. The officers leaned in unconsciously, as though they could hear him better that way.

"I neglected to tell Mr. Moton the pistol was a Barretta 92F, the same model used by Mel Gibson's character Martin Riggs in the *Lethal Weapon* movies. I see you carry a Sig Sauer, Officer, though I assume the detective uses something smaller and more concealable. A Glock 23 is standard issue." Colin focused his attention on the detective. "Those are very popular with gang-intervention officers."

The detective froze. "I didn't tell you I was with gang intervention."

"You used to have a spiderweb tattoo on your neck, which symbolizes a struggle to turn your life around. I assume you succeeded, since you had it removed and joined the LAPD. Yet your knowledge of and contact with the criminal underworld perfectly suit you to work on gang-related cases. Also, you thought someone may be intimidating me, which means you suspect a gang connection to the shooting."

There was another very long silence from both police officers.

"I see," the detective replied.

"I didn't see any gang members in the cafeteria before the shooting," Colin offered sadly. "But I haven't finished mapping the school's overlapping social networks, so I suppose it's possible. Would you like me to show you my chart when I'm finished?"

"That won't be necessary," the uniformed officer said. He looked at the detective, who shrugged in a way that reminded Colin of his father. "I think we're good here."

Dinnertime at the Fischer house was considered sacrosanct.

Mrs. Fischer had insisted for as long as Colin could remember that dinner wasn't just a time to eat, but a time to communicate. She seemed unimpressed by Colin's insistence that speaking and eating at the same time made both take longer, although she conceded that at no time would anyone be required to speak with his mouth full. This seemed to placate him and partly explained why Colin chewed slowly, carefully, and constantly. The rest was explained by Colin's insistence that it was good for digestion.

As a result, Colin communicated very little during meals. It wasn't unusual for him to spend the entire time dishing large helpings of food onto his plate (divided into their own sectors, which weren't allowed to touch) and say little more than "please," "thank you," or "excuse me." Tonight was no different.

What was very different was the tension in the air as Colin tucked into a plate of lemon chicken and savory rice. Dinner was on the table early that night. An emergency community meeting had been called at West Valley High School so Dr. Doran could address what she called "the crisis." Colin's father wasn't even home yet.

Danny was buzzing with the news of the day. To him, it was the most exciting thing that had ever happened anywhere. "I heard it was a point forty-four magnum," he chirped, "and that some dude was shooting at the lunch lady—"

"Enough," his mother snapped. Danny fell quiet. Colin could see she was WORRIED. Usually, his mother attempted to disguise emotions she thought might upset her sons. The fact that she wasn't even trying in this case was very interesting.

Colin was chewing his last bite of chicken and carrying his plate to the sink when his father appeared at the back door. Mr. Fischer didn't look WORRIED, but ANGRY. Then he saw Colin and smiled. It took Colin a moment to identify his father's RELIEF.

"Hey, buddy," Mr. Fischer said.

"Hello," Colin said, dutifully rinsing his dirty dishes and placing them into the dishwasher rack.

Mrs. Fischer checked her watch. "We're gonna be late."

"Best I could do," he answered.

"I know your team is under the gun." She winced, realizing what she just said. "Sorry, bad choice of words."

"Are you kidding?" Mr. Fischer heaped food onto

a plate. "I spent half the day telling everybody Colin wasn't involved."

"Can I go out back now?" Colin asked. He very much wanted to put in some trampoline time before the assembly. There was thinking to be done.

Mrs. Fischer checked her watch again. She was a project manager at NASA, and Colin knew that time mattered to her differently than it did to most people. "Fifteen minutes. Then we've gotta go."

The door slammed shut as Colin disappeared into the backyard.

"He *wasn't* involved, was he?" Mr. Fischer asked.

"God, no."

Through the open kitchen window, Colin popped into view. He seemed to hover in midair a moment, then dropped back out of sight.

"Do I have to go?" Danny asked. His shoulders slumped.

"Five minutes ago, this was the most exciting thing you'd ever heard," Mrs. Fischer reminded him.

Colin popped up again, this time with his feet splayed out in front of him—an unstable configuration. He tumbled slightly as he disappeared.

"Guns are exciting," Danny explained. "Talking about them isn't."

In the backyard, Colin bounced rhythmically on his trampoline. *Up-down . . . Up-down . . .* His parents and

Danny went in and out of sight, their voices muted but audible. To Colin, it was as if the kitchen window were a television screen, and he could watch his family on it. He closed his eyes. For a moment there was only the darkness and the soft, regular squeak of the trampoline springs.

Up-down, up-down . . .

Images from the day flashed through Colin's mind like a slideshow, in time with every launch from the surface of the trampoline: a basketball, sailing through the air . . . Mr. Gates, writing equations on the blackboard . . . The gentle curve of Melissa's body, as she wrote in his Notebook . . . Mouths chewing food . . .

And the handgun, lying abandoned on the cafeteria floor.

From the kitchen, Mr. Fischer absently watched his son leap higher and higher. "Maybe we could dust off those old NASA plans for a moon colony and ship Colin and Danny there until graduation," he mused.

"Send Colin first," Danny muttered, finally finished with his dinner.

"I made five free throws!"—Colin suddenly exclaimed at his father, shouting to be heard as he leaped upward—"and three perimeter shots"—as he went down again—"today in PE!" He let himself settle into a standing position. "Mr. Turrentine says I have a killer jump shot!" Colin stopped to catch his breath.

For a moment, Mr. Fischer just looked at Colin, as though he didn't understand what he'd just heard. Then he burst into laughter and stepped outside:

"You played *basketball*?"

The parking lot of West Valley High was filled with cars, ranging from expensive SUVs to thirty-year-old Japanese imports held together with wire. As Colin climbed out of the back of his father's Audi (which, per his request, had been parked in the first available spot), he produced his Notebook and a fresh green-ink pen and began to write:

> 7:58 P.M. West Valley High School parking lot. School almost as busy as during the day, except more because there are an average of 1.6 parents per student. Auditorium will be crowded, loud. Probably smelly.

Colin was right on all three counts.

He disliked auditoriums immensely because of the crowds, the smell, and the noise. Over time, he'd learned to deal with them by closing his eyes, breathing through his mouth, and allowing the discordant voices to meld into white noise. This was more difficult to pull off during an awards ceremony because Colin was invariably asked to stand and be recognized for his citizenship, effort, or academic achievement. However, if he moved as quickly as possible to the stage and back to his seat, it wasn't too bad.

Dr. Doran had been addressing parents, teachers, and a smattering of students for almost ten minutes, offering the obligatory empathy, assurances, and calls for unity—most of which Colin had tuned out. His mind was exploring more important matters. Specifically, he wondered who owned the gun, who had been careless enough to drop it on the floor, and if they were indeed one and the same person.

"As long as everybody stays cool," Dr. Doran concluded, "we'll all be just fine."

Colin heard the low buzz of voices, indicating side conversations beginning among the crowd. His own parents just looked at each other, although Colin found it difficult to decipher the meaning of their furrowed brows.

"So that's it?" A woman's voice carried above the noise of the crowd.

Colin sat up straighter, so he could see where the question had come from. He needn't have bothered; the woman rose from her seat, unbidden. "A few touchy-feely seminars, a week of cops on campus, and you hope this all goes away?" she asked.

Dr. Doran considered the woman carefully, and Colin saw his principal's eyes lock in on the boy seated beside her: Rudy Moore.

Rudy was dressed in a pressed, button-down oxford

and a conservative silk tie. His hair was damp, indicating that he'd taken a shower between the end of school and the beginning of the assembly. Colin found this strange but couldn't put his finger on why.

"I assure you," Dr. Doran replied evenly, "we take this very seriously. However, I would remind you that West Valley High had the best safety record in the district until this incident."

Rudy beckoned his mother to lean down and whispered in her ear. Mrs. Moore looked back at Dr. Doran. "You mean last year, when someone else was principal."

An uncomfortable silence fell over the auditorium. Dr. Doran appeared to be formulating a careful response when Colin's father stood up to take the floor.

"Look," Mr. Fischer said, "I don't know about last year or any other principals. That's not the issue here, and it's not useful to suggest that it is."

He aimed that last comment squarely at Mrs. Moore. She glared back coldly.

"But talking about how things were up until this incident is like saying the *Titanic* had the best safety record in the Atlantic until she hit the iceberg."[7]

Laughter rippled through the crowd. Even Dr.

---

[7] The RMS *Titanic* sank on April 14, 1912, after a collision with an iceberg in the North Atlantic, killing 1,517 passengers. Since the collision occurred during the ship's maiden voyage, her safety record was technically spotless prior to the incident. This made little difference to the victims.

Doran smiled. Colin saw his mother smiling too—but her smile was different from Dr. Doran's or anyone else's. She was not AMUSED, but PROUD.

"Even one isolated incident is too many," he continued. "It's a miracle that bullet ended up in the ceiling and not in a child's body."

Murmurs of agreement met Colin's ears as other parents began to take their cue from Rudy's mother and Mr. Fischer.

"We all know where this kind of thing comes from," one angry father blurted out. "It's the values these kids are learning from the TV and video games, 'cause nobody is teaching them at home!"

Someone's mother chimed in her agreement. "Yeah, I don't spend two hours a day driving between a job I hate and a house I can't afford for this! We moved here to get away from the kind of people who do this."

Behind Colin, a man hurled back, "And what 'kind of people' might those be?"

Colin huddled tightly against himself like a turtle. He could feel the tension in the room escalate around him. His heartbeat picked up speed.

Mrs. Fischer looked at her son, careful not to touch him given his current emotional state. "Colin," she said quietly but crisply as people around her began to bark out opinions in a cacophony of fear, anger, and resentment, "do you need to get out of here?"

Colin shook his head. *No.* He was determined to see

this through, even though it was obvious even to him where it was leading: *shouting*.

It was obvious to Dr. Doran too. "Let's be clear about something," she said. Her voice boomed from the speakers, drowning out the crowd with a whine of feedback. "This didn't happen to one or a few of us. It happened to all of us. As a community. We need to respond as a community." She had the crowd's attention again, and she seized it. "Anyone who can't handle that is welcome to leave. Seriously—go home."

Colin recognized this as a bold, risky stratagem. In his experience, parents didn't like to be told they weren't in charge—especially when they weren't. However, it seemed to work.

"No takers?" Dr. Doran asked. "Good. Let's talk about how we're going to fix this and make sure it never, ever happens again."

Mrs. Fischer elbowed her husband in the ribs. "She can stay," she said.

Dr. Doran continued. "First, I've asked the police to run random sweeps through campus for the indefinite future. We're very confident—"

"And when do you plan to catch the little thug who brought the gun?" Mrs. Moore interrupted.

Rudy stared at Dr. Doran. His eyes made Colin think of a doll's, not just because of his association with the Case of the Talking Doll, but because there was something wrong about them. Something not quite alive.

Regardless, Colin hated dolls—the more "realistic" the mold, the less he liked them.[8]

Dr. Doran fell quiet again. She wrinkled her nose. It reminded Colin of the woman Samantha from the old TV show *Bewitched*, which he had watched dutifully on cable until he gave up television altogether after learning of the "Tommy Westphall Hypothesis." The hypothesis held that the vast majority of American television takes place in the mind of an autistic boy featured in the series finale of *St. Elsewhere*. Marie had exposed Colin to the idea in an attempt to illustrate how things that seem to have no connection can have subtle links that bring everything together in amusing, wonderful ways. This was not at all how Colin interpreted the revelation. For Colin, imaginary stories about imaginary stories were one step too far removed from reality.[9] Still, he'd always liked Samantha.

---

8 Japanese roboticist Masahiro Mori coined the term "uncanny valley" to describe how, as an object became more and more human-looking, it reached a point where it provoked fear and revulsion in a human observer instead of empathy. Other researchers hypothesized this phenomenon might trace to a genetic imperative to avoid diseased or dead members of one's own species. Whatever its cause, computer animators have been aware of the uncanny valley since 1988, when audiences watching Pixar's short film *Tin Toy* were charmed by the titular windup character but horrified by the film's animated human infant.

9 In the closing moments of the *St. Elsewhere* series finale, the boy (Tommy Westphall) is shown holding a snow globe containing the hospital in which the show was set. The image strongly suggests Tommy had imagined every character and situation. Because of an unusual and intricate web of connections between characters (from crossovers and writer references on subsequent programs) it could be inferred that

"I can't give you a name yet. But we do have one," she said.

Mr. Fischer rose again. "I don't need a name, ma'am," he said, "Just do me and my son a favor: Whoever it was, please nail him, her, or it to the wall."

Colin could see his father was very SERIOUS, although he was intrigued by the reference to an "it." Over the years, Colin had come to realize his parents tended toward sensational, figurative language to make a point. This was probably one of those times.

Dr. Doran nodded solemnly, then stepped out from the podium. Her thumb and forefinger formed a "0." It meant:

"Zero. Tolerance."

Applause erupted from the audience, endorsing the principal's get-tough attitude. Colin just wished they could have endorsed her more quietly.

The next day, West Valley High School buzzed with response to Dr. Doran's big meeting. Everywhere Colin went, people talked about her closing pronouncements to the exclusion of nearly everything else.

In the hallway, Abby told Melissa with CONCERN, "Did you hear? They're gonna try him as an adult. . . ."

---

other shows were constructs of Tommy's expansive imagination. This list includes such notables as *M*A*S*H*, *Law & Order*, and *The X-Files*, and continues to add to itself.

". . . *Zero tolerance* . . ." Eddie repeated to Stan, GRAVE.

". . . because the cops found three boxes of ammo in his locker," an ASTONISHED Cooper revealed to a gaggle in study hall, just after the bell. Colin didn't know if this was true or not, but doubted Cooper would have this information. Colin said nothing.

Instead, he sat in study hall and wrote in his Notebook:

> Wayne Connelly is not in school today. He is the unnamed suspect.

Melissa approached and took a seat next to Colin. "Hello, Melissa," he said. "How are you today?"

"Okay, I guess," she replied. "I mean, wow. What a day, right?"

Colin stared at her blankly, concerned that he had missed her meaning.

"Yesterday. The gun?"

"Oh, the gun," Colin said. "Very interesting."

She tossed her hair. It smelled like strawberries. Colin liked strawberries. "It was interesting all right." Melissa smiled at him. It was not a smile Colin recognized, but he felt no compulsion to look away and refer to his cheat sheet. "That was really brave of you, how you were the only one who didn't run. Weren't you scared at all?"

"No," Colin replied. "Everyone was running away, so whoever fired the gun must have stopped."

She peered at his Notebook. Colin generally made it a point to guard its contents, but once again his reaction ran counter to his usual instincts. He focused instead on the spray of light freckles across Melissa's nose. Suddenly, Colin developed an inexplicable craving for strawberry shortcake—which seemed odd, given its mushy texture.

Melissa looked at him, having read the page. Multiple emotions rippled across her face, too fast and too mixed up for Colin to lock in on any one of them.

"Wayne Connelly?" she asked.

"He isn't in school today."

"He's been a creep and a bully since we were all in kindergarten, but I never thought he'd actually shoot someone." Melissa fell silent for a moment. She looked away from Colin. Her face scrunched up a little. Then she turned back to him with a frown. "I guess he won't be crashing any more parties to steal my cake, huh?"

Colin blinked. "*Cake*," he said. He considered this word for a very long time. When he looked up again, Melissa was gone.

Colin scribbled furiously in his Notebook, then gathered his books and went for the door. The study hall monitor stopped him. His name was Mr. Bell, and he taught band. Band was a subject Colin endeavored to avoid at all costs.

"Colin," Mr. Bell said, "where are you going?"

"Dr. Doran told me if I ever needed to see her, I would be excused from class. She said I wouldn't be told 'no.'"

And then Colin hurried away, deaf to Mr. Bell's protests.

Dr. Doran looked up from a stack of papers as Colin marched into her office unannounced and wordlessly took a seat.

"I'm a little busy at the moment," she said. "And by the way, you should be in class right now."

"Yes," Colin answered. All of these things appeared to be true. "But it's very important I tell you first that Wayne Connelly is innocent."

Dr. Doran's nose wrinkled. Colin took note of it.

"What makes you think Wayne Connelly is even a suspect?"

Colin pointed to a chair in the corner of the office. "The stack of schoolbooks and homework in the corner with Wayne's name and address on them. They suggest he's been suspended but not actually arrested or charged with a crime yet."

Dr. Doran flicked her eyes toward the chair, then back to Colin. "Okay, I'll bite. Is there something you didn't tell the police when they interviewed you?"

"No. I described everything that I thought was important at the time. But what I didn't realize then was the importance of the cake."

"The cake?"

"Yes, the cake. The pistol grip of the gun was smeared with frosting, but Wayne Connelly eats very neatly. So you see? The gun couldn't have been his." Colin took Dr. Doran's silence to be an acknowledgment of his hypothesis. "We have to tell the investigating authorities," he insisted.

She wrinkled her nose again, just as she had when confronted with the trick cell phone, and just as she had at the assembly. He was beginning to detect a pattern. "There is no 'we' here, Colin. This is a police investigation, not mine. Or *yours*."

"But you heard what I said about the cake—"

"And I'll be sure to pass it on. Until then, ask my secretary to write you a note for your teacher on the way out."

"Dr. Doran, I—"

"*Colin*. Enough. You're a student, not a detective. Are we clear?"

Colin considered this for a very long moment, deciding against suggesting that she had just asserted a false dichotomy.[10] "Yes," he said.

On his way out the door, he stopped. There was one

---

[10] A false dichotomy occurs when two ideas are presented as mutually exclusive, but are in fact perfectly compatible. For example: "You can have either peanut butter or you can have chocolate" is a false dichotomy. This is most easily demonstrated by the Reese's Peanut Butter Cup. Peanut Butter Cups were Colin's favorite example, because proving chocolate and peanut butter go together was always delicious.

last thing he wanted to share. "Dr. Doran?" he asked carefully.

"Yes, Colin?"

"You wrinkle your nose when you know something and you don't want to say it."

Colin excused himself without another word.

Colin strode down the empty hallway, not even bothering to count his steps as his pen moved furiously across a blank page of his Notebook:

> Wayne Connelly is innocent, and I will prove it.
> The game is afoot.

CHAPTER SEVEN:
THE BATTLESHIP POTEMKIN

Our neighbors once witnessed me take a metal mixing bowl and some household chemicals into the garage. After hearing a loud bang, they called the police, assuming I was attempting to manufacture drugs—a not uncommon activity on the fringes of the San Fernando Valley. What the neighbors didn't know and my father eventually confirmed for the police was the truth: I was trying to work out the principles of explosive pulse propulsion in spaceflight for a science project. The police laughed, although my father made me spend a month's allowance to replace the bowl.

The misunderstanding that arose from my experiment with rocketry was in many ways an echo of the consequences of Kuleshov's experiments with film. His work sparked a revolution in filmmaking because the implication of his results went far beyond the meaning of facial expressions. Kuleshov demonstrated that when you present images together, the audience connects them whether they're actually related or not. Sergei Eisenstein proved this when he cut old stock footage of British naval maneuvers into "The Battleship Potemkin," a film he shot entirely on land.

Audiences assumed Eisenstein had shot it on the ocean. When Western diplomats saw this, they sent coded telegrams to their governments, relaying their horrifying discovery that the Soviets had secretly built a new navy. As a result, untold national resources were diverted in response to an escalation that existed only in a scene in a movie in which their own ships stood in for their enemy's.

Without realizing it, Kuleshov confirmed a long-held belief about the best way to deceive people: Show them things they want to believe. The rest will take care of itself.

Mrs. Fischer had been taking Colin to the shopping mall in Woodland Hills since he was a small boy. It began as a part of Colin's therapy, meant to help him slowly overcome his fear of new places. "Like putting the frog in the pot of water and boiling it slowly," his mother used to joke.[11]

---

11 The oft-told story is that a frog tossed into a pot of boiling water will leap out immediately, while a frog in a pot of water where the temperature

At first, they merely drove into the mall's parking lot, where they would sit until returning home. After a month, Mrs. Fischer convinced Colin to walk to the front doors and touch them. The automatic glass doors presented a terrifying and impassable barrier for nearly a year, until his mother produced an article from the Internet that satisfied Colin he was in no danger of being chopped in half while crossing the threshold.

Now, the mall offered familiarity and comfort to Colin, as long as he avoided the row of electronics stores along a particular first-floor promenade or the talking snowmen on display during the Christmas season. Colin's mother knew the drill. With a "Meet us at the west entrance in forty-five minutes," she dropped Danny off to check out video games and took Colin to find the gym clothes and shoes he suddenly insisted he needed.

They ended up in a second-floor sporting goods shop where the clerks wore striped shirts meant to evoke the uniform of a football referee. Colin knew the exact brand, model number, and color of the shoes he wanted based on reviews on the Internet and an

---

is turned up slowly will not notice the change and sit contentedly until it dies. This is not actually true. Frogs are actually quite sensitive to changes in temperature and will hop out of a pot the moment it becomes uncomfortably warm. Colin once got in an argument with a middle school science teacher over this very fact and offered to prove his point with a large flask, a Bunsen burner, and a live frog. Instead, his teacher consulted Wikipedia before grudgingly accepting Colin's assertion.

article in *Consumer Reports*, and so he resisted the clerk's attempts to sell him a more expensive shoe. "It's what all the pro hoops players are wearing this year," the clerk explained to Colin and his mother, as though he were confiding state secrets.

"Oh," Colin said. On one hand, professional basketball players were presumably experts in shoe dynamics and durability. On the other, they tended to wear the shoe of whichever manufacturer paid the most endorsement money. In the end, Colin fell back on practicality. "I'm not a professional hoops player," he explained. "I just take gym."

Defeated, the salesclerk disappeared to the back room to retrieve the requested shoe in Colin's size, while Mrs. Fischer thumbed through racks of 100 percent cotton T-shirts and shorts. Colin took the time available to him to watch the flow of the traffic through the mall. The walkway was sculpted and landscaped to suggest a narrow canyon. The doors and display windows were even designed to evoke Anasazi cliff dwellings.[12]

---

12 It was a long-held belief that the ancient Anasazi people of the American Southwest were peace-loving farmers. That belief had to be reassessed when archaeological digs around Anasazi population centers unearthed clear evidence of cannibalism. In fact, the word *anasazii* itself is a Navajo term, translating roughly to "ancient enemy." The Navajo and other neighboring tribes considered the Anasazi dangerous sorcerers and shapeshifters, as well as taking issue with their rather particular culinary habits. Colin found the whole idea of cannibalism distasteful—it was hard enough just to kiss his grandmother.

Colin mentally cataloged the different subgroups within the space—speed-walking senior citizens, mothers with toddlers at the indoor play area, bored teens lounging in knots. It reminded him of his high school's cafeteria and how it, too, used geography to sort its inhabitants into smaller units. Unfortunately, the scuffle between Wayne and Eddie just before the gun went off scrambled those different social groups together, making it nearly impossible to narrow down the origin of the weapon.

From this vantage point, Colin had an excellent view of the entrance to a large department store. In spite of the high-quality people-watching opportunities it offered, he disliked this particular store. Cosmetics and perfumes were positioned near the front, forcing Colin to walk through a fog of fragrances every time he entered or left.

A slender, blonde female form stood at the cosmetics counter, her back turned. Colin considered the shape of her back, and for a moment he perked up in hope that it might be Melissa. Then the girl turned to show her mother the melon-colored lipstick she'd just applied, and Colin sank. The girl was not Melissa, but Sandy Ryan.

"Colin?" his mother asked. It took him a moment to realize she had finished buying the shoes and gym clothes and was ready to go. In spite of his mother's insistence that it be used efficiently and that there was never enough of it, Colin was increasingly convinced that time was entirely subjective.[13]

They headed out just as Sandy and her mother exited the department store with a bag of cosmetics. A brief and unwelcome exchange of pleasantries seemed inevitable. Sandy's mother and Mrs. Fischer had known each for many years. Colin knew the only way to avert social catastrophe would be for the two women not to see each other, and lacking a readily available distraction, that seemed an unlikely outcome. Accepting this, he prepared for the ensuing awkwardness by opening the bag containing his new shoes and staring at them as if they were bugs under a very large magnifying glass.

"Susan Fischer!" Sandy's mother squeaked.

"Allison Ryan," Mrs. Fischer replied.

"Terrible what happened at school, isn't it?"

"Oh, don't get me started . . ."

Sandy shifted from foot to foot, looking around as though she had no idea her mother was engaged in this conversation. She blushed, obviously EMBARRASSED. Colin surmised this was motivated at least in part by

---

13 Or, as was once noted in the 1985 science-fiction film *The Adventures of Buckaroo Banzai across the Eighth Dimension,* "The reason for time is so everything doesn't happen at once." Colin liked this movie a great deal, mainly because his father took such enjoyment out of it. Even so, he quibbled with the realism of a hero who was a quantum physicist, a rock star, a surgeon, and a ninja all at once. Surely, no human being could know so much about so many different things.

a well-documented need for teenagers—especially girls—to pretend their parents and their parents' friends don't exist as social animals. However, it was impossible to be sure. Colin reached for his Notebook.

As he flipped to a blank page and glanced up, Colin made direct but unintentional eye contact with Sandy. The sensation was alarming and physically uncomfortable, like all the blood in his limbs was draining from him at once. Colin looked away, nonetheless aware that Sandy's adolescent awkwardness had blossomed into outright HOSTILITY.

It hadn't always been this way. Once, when they were young children, Colin and Sandy were almost friends. They went to preschool together. Their mothers drove them back and forth each day, each in turn. One afternoon, Sandy's mother was caught in traffic, and Mrs. Fischer helpfully brought Sandy home to play with Colin. Colin invited Sandy to his room, where he announced they would complete the suspension bridge he had been building entirely out of Legos. Colin's mother was thrilled.

All was quiet for an hour. Mrs. Fischer had just begun to entertain visions of a budding friendship and regular playdates, when a piercing scream shattered the peace that had settled on the house. She pounded up the stairs and threw open the door to find Sandy asleep on Colin's bed, lying in a puddle of her own urine. The scream had come from Colin, whose carefully ordered space had been violated in a most horrifying way. The carpool ended shortly thereafter.

"Whoever it was, I hope they find him," Sandy's mother said. "I hope they try him as an adult, put him in a dark hole, and throw away the key."

"Why does there have to be a key?" Mrs. Fischer agreed.

"Actually," Colin said with a frown. "I'd like to go back and try the compression tops. I think I'd find the pressure on my long nerves calming." He studiously avoided looking at Sandy. It was as if he and his mother were the only people in the mall.

Mrs. Fischer sighed heavily, then offered Mrs. Ryan a wan smile. "Gotta calm those nerves," she said.

"I hear you," Mrs. Ryan agreed conspiratorially. "But I prefer wine."

"Later, Allison," Mrs. Fischer said with a smile, turning with Colin back toward the athletic store.

"Call me sometime," Mrs. Ryan said. "We should get the kids together."

"Ugh," Sandy said behind them. It was the closest she and Colin had come to a real conversation since they were four years old. They moved in different circles now, even if the bed-wetting incident didn't hang over them every time they met. It occurred to Colin that any social map he might have constructed as a toddler in preschool would look very different from the one he imagined now. Indeed, the labels, connections, and groups he identified—his whole taxonomy—might be entirely mutable. The insight reinforced Colin's conviction that he needed an efficient, physical method of tracking it all.

"Mom," he said, "could we stop by the arts and crafts store on the way out?"

A few minutes later, Mrs. Fischer and Colin exited the mall. Danny slouched against an exterior wall adjoining the parking lot, talking to a pair of boys who appeared to be his own age. Colin did not know their names. "I thought I said meet us *inside* the west entrance," Mrs. Fischer said. By *thought,* Colin knew his mother meant *did,* although he wasn't certain she was recalling her own instructions accurately.

"You said *at,*" Danny protested as he loped over. "Here I am."

Mrs. Fischer wasn't used to back talk, and her suddenly narrowed, suspicious eyes indicated she was in no mood to get comfortable with it now. Colin once described this oft-used expression to Marie, who agreed it didn't correspond neatly to any of the ones on Colin's cheat sheet. They decided to dub it MOM FACE. The name had stuck.

"Danny is right," Colin piped up, breaking the standoff. "*At* the west entrance could technically mean either inside or outside the doors."

Colin's mother laughed. Danny turned his head away, inexplicably ANNOYED. "Stop helping," he said, and trudged off toward the car.

Hefting his bags of art supplies and athletic shoes, Colin followed. He puzzled over the meaning of Danny's request. After all, Colin hadn't been trying to help anyone—he was just pointing out the facts. Who the truth helped and how much was irrelevant.

Colin disappeared immediately into his room, shoes and shirts under one arm, art supplies under the other. He had concluded that building an effective social map of West Valley High wasn't just a matter of comfort and survival, but was critical to determining the actual owner of the gun that so explosively disrupted Melissa's birthday party.

From his laptop, Colin accessed the high school's website and printed out a class list, circling the names of students he thought were most relevant and interesting to the case. Nearly all of them had their own pages on social-networking sites, so Colin found their profile pictures and printed them out in turn. With the stack of photos before him, Colin tacked each one carefully to the cork board above his desk.

One photo was missing from the group: Wayne Connelly.

> Wayne Connelly seems to have no online presence. There are no photos and no dedicated social-networking pages. It is as if Wayne does not exist. Is this by design or simply an inconvenient

coincidence? Perhaps some combination? The absence of references to Wayne on other students' pages indicates social isolation, or vast conspiracy. Investigate.

Colin leafed through his eighth-grade yearbook, looking for a physical photo of Wayne, but was stymied once more. Evidently, Wayne had been absent on photo day that year or he had skillfully avoided the photographer. With a thoughtful frown, Colin took a black triangle of paper and labeled it WAYNE CONNELLY. It would have to do.

With color-coded sticky tabs purchased at the art supplies store, Colin categorized the various students by their social, academic, geographic, and socioeconomic cliques. Lengths of colored yarn indicated connections between individuals and groups, further broken down by relationship type: friendship, romance, rivalry. Colin did this all in conscious imitation of the boards used by the FBI and other law enforcement agencies to track links between the members of Mafia families and other criminal conspiracies. He found the process almost as useful as the product—physical manipulation of real objects, even when they represented ideas or abstractions, helped Colin to think about them.

Colin regarded the final product with a frown. Its precision was marred by the paper triangle standing in for Wayne. The lack of a photo in arguably the most important spot stood out in the field of smiling profile photos. Colin worried the visual effect could bias his analysis and so made a note to find a more suitable representation.

As Colin crawled into bed, he saw that he had positioned his social map next to his photograph of Basil Rathbone. It gave the effect of Holmes himself pondering the mystery. Colin found this comforting and wondered what the Great Detective might say about it all. He was certain that Holmes would have solved the whole thing by now.

Then Colin eased into sleep, dreaming of fog and night and gaslit streets.

The next morning, Colin stood on the blacktop of West Valley High in his new compression tops, slowly dribbling a basketball and thinking about lines.

He felt the lines on the basketball under his fingers as he rhythmically bounced it—two circles bounding the sphere like an equator and international date line, two ellipses covering the tiny planet's north and south poles. On the blacktop itself, lines demarcated the borders of the half-court basketball arena. They had been repainted several times, the paint fading from endless hours of sun, rain, and teenage feet, but the new never quite aligned with the old. The imprecision of it bothered Colin greatly, as though the lines were merely suggestions and not hard boundaries, so he tried instead to concentrate on the soothing metronome of the bouncing basketball.

"Hey Colin, isn't it a little early for Halloween?"

Cooper and Eddie stood before him. Cooper had asked the question with a grin Colin couldn't place. Colin was about to agree that indeed, October 31 was nearly two months away, when he realized Cooper was actually referring to the orange-and-black colors of Colin's T-shirt. His question was therefore *rhetorical*, the recognition of which would have made Marie proud. She had drilled Colin for hours in the difficult art of distinguishing literal statements ("You look nice today") from metaphorical, idiomatic ones ("You make a better door than a window"). This seemed to qualify.

"These are the school colors of the California Institute of Technology," Colin explained. "I got this when I went with my father to an alumni event."

Cooper and Eddie shrugged. Obviously, neither was familiar with the athletic history of Caltech.[14] However, since Cooper wore a USC Trojans jersey and Eddie a Notre Dame tank top, they could understand adorning oneself in a parent's school colors.

"So anyway," Cooper continued, "we saw you hit those baskets yesterday."

---

14 Understandable, since Caltech is widely regarded as the worst athletic school in NCAA Division III, a fact Colin's father pretended not to care about.

As far as Colin knew, these last two sentences represented the most Cooper had ever spoken to him at one time in years. Did this mean they had developed a rapport? Colin hoped so. Cooper was friends with most of the participants in yesterday's brawl and was therefore a potentially valuable source of information for the investigation.

"Thank you, Cooper," Colin replied. "Could I ask you a few questions about—"

"The thing is," Eddie said, abruptly cutting Colin off, "we were wondering if you'd play for us. Three on three."

"Play what for you?" Colin had never been asked a question like this before.

Cooper laughed. "Basketball, short—*dude*. We want you to play on our team."

Dude was an all-purpose slang term that often denoted affection, a decided promotion from the insensitive and pejorative *shortbus*. Colin absorbed the change.

It certainly sounded as though the boys were inviting him into their social circle. This was exciting because it meant they might be willing to talk to him about The Case of the Birthday Cake and the Gun.

"Yeah, whattaya say?" Eddie pressed.

"Then you can ask whatever you want," Cooper added.

"I'll be back shortly," Colin said.

He marched past three different games of three-on-three half-court basketball and noted with apprehension the fouling, trash-talking, and rough-housing that accompanied the play. Colin scanned the area for Mr. Turrentine but didn't see him anywhere.

"Fischer," Mr. Turrentine said, standing beside him. He seemed to come out of nowhere, but it occurred to Colin that Mr. Turrentine might have been there the whole time. Colin wondered idly how a man as old as Mr. Turrentine could move so quietly, but more immediate concerns needed to be addressed.

"Mr. Turrentine?"

"Yes, Fischer."

"Does basketball involve a lot of physical contact?"

Mr. Turrentine fixed his gaze on Colin for what felt like a very long time, during which Colin tried to be polite and maintain eye contact. The intense stare reminded Colin of one of his favorite mystery stories: *The Thirty-Nine Steps*,[15] by John Buchan. Buchan described the story's villain as having "eyes hooded like a hawk's." Colin had always thought that statement a hyperbolic one, but Mr. Turrentine's strangely hooded eyes indeed suggested an observant bird of prey.

"Are you a little china doll, Fischer?" Mr. Turrentine

---

15 *The Thirty-Nine Steps* was adapted into a movie in 1935 by Alfred Hitchcock. The film took several liberties with the book, including substituting the character of Annabelle for a man named Franklin Scudder. Colin's father surmised this was most likely to add "romantic tension" for the female audience. However, he could not explain why Hitchcock thought women wouldn't appreciate a perfectly good story just as it was.

asked. "Are you afraid you might break? Because you don't look like a little china doll to me."

Colin recognized this, too, as a rhetorical question—Mr. Turrentine seemed fond of them. But truth be told, Colin only identified this one because Mr. Turrentine had helpfully supplied the answer himself.

"No," said Colin. "I'm not a little china doll. I just don't like to be touched unless I'm asked first."

"Me neither, but life is a contact sport and pads are not an option." Mr. Turrentine's raptor eyes gave away nothing. "It's not football. You'll be fine."

With that, he turned his attention to a game in progress. Colin remained dubious about the prospect of playing basketball, his concern counterbalanced by the enticement of getting to question Cooper and Eddie. He walked back to them.

"I'm ready to play."

The opposing team consisted of Stan and two of his equally large, muscular friends. For a moment, Colin hesitated. On one hand, the presence of another eyewitness to the gun incident was a stroke of good fortune. On the other hand, playing against the notoriously cruel, short-tempered Stan was not.

Colin observed carefully as the game began, trying to imitate Cooper and Eddie's bobbing, wide-legged stances. Stan covered Eddie, slapping at him and trying to force him out of bounds until Eddie quickly fed the ball to Colin, left open as Stan's friends had run to cover the tall and obviously dangerous Cooper.

The ball stung his fingertips but stuck in place. Colin stared down at it, mesmerized by the patterned stripes. "Shoot it!" Eddie hollered across the court.

Colin obeyed. He shot two-handed, thinking as it sailed through the air that its parabolic arc evoked the elliptical stripes of the ball itself. He was pondering whether or not the similarity was a coincidence as the ball sailed cleanly through the basket.

"Good one!" shouted Cooper, visibly *EXCITED*. Stan's arms flopped to his sides in disbelief, reminding Colin of a marionette whose strings had suddenly been cut. "Two points for the man!"

As Cooper and Eddie ran to take up defensive positions, Cooper playfully slapped Colin on the shoulder. Colin cringed and recoiled, suppressing the urge to scream and strike back. After all, he reasoned, the other boy was only trying to congratulate him.

"Please don't do that," Colin said, his voice tighter and flatter than usual. "Or warn me first."

Cooper put his hands up and backed away from Colin. "Fine."

It was a statement, not a judgment. Like everyone who had gone to school with Colin for several years, Cooper was aware of Colin's idiosyncrasies—even if he didn't understand them.

None of this went unnoticed by Stan. He nudged

his two teammates, miming a shove. The boys nodded in affirmation of their silent, spontaneous conspiracy.

The game resumed. Cooper stripped the ball from one of Stan's teammates, and the teams switched positions. This time, Stan moved to cover Colin, hanging back while Cooper passed Colin the ball.

Stan matched Colin's stride, expertly anticipating his clumsy attempts at evasion for a clear shot. Stan's long arms shot outward. He slapped at Colin's shirt and elbows, reaching for the ball.

"Don't," said Colin between breaths. "Please don't do that."

Too late. Stan stole the ball and took it into the paint for an easy basket. Colin watched, attempting to identify his emotions. Anger and fear he knew well, but another unfamiliar feeling had presented itself: disappointment. In that moment, Colin realized something very important about himself. He didn't like to lose.

Cooper jogged up to him. "Don't let Stan get in your head," he said quietly, trying to be SUPPORTIVE. "That's what he wants."

A few seconds later, Eddie took the ball and checked it straight to Colin. Colin dribbled, trying to keep his free arm in front as a defensive shield, but it didn't matter. No matter which way Colin turned, Stan was in his face.

Cooper and Eddie watched the dance, FRUSTRATED

and growing ANNOYED. There was no official twenty-four-second shot clock in half-court three-on-three, but holding the ball for extended periods was still frowned upon.

"Come on, you're open," called Eddie. Colin was beyond that now. Stan's harassment had flustered him too much to shoot, locking him into an endlessly repeating pattern—*step forward, feint, step back*—like an old vinyl record with a scratch repeating the same musical phrase over and over again. Colin finally broke the impasse and fed the ball to Eddie. But Eddie was too well-guarded. He flicked the ball back to Colin.

"Just *shoot*," Eddie implored.

Stan stepped in front of Colin. He smiled, checking the playground for Mr. Turrentine. At that moment, the teacher was on the opposite side, helping an obese boy develop his jump shot. Satisfied, Stan turned back to Colin. He smiled again. SMUG.

Colin watched Stan's feet. He had detected a pattern in Stan's back-and-forth defensive weaving—a pattern he could learn and defeat by darting past him to a clear shooting position. It was a good plan, one that probably would have worked had Colin in that moment not felt a sudden searing pain in his left arm. Stan dug his hand into Colin's wrist, his thumb stabbing the spot where nerve tissue ran close to the bone, a juncture that martial artists referred to as a "pressure point."[16]

As Colin dropped the ball and Stan reached to take it, Colin released a hoarse, animalistic howl of pain and rage. The sound was terrifying. So terrifying, in fact, that it stunned Stan into inaction long enough for Colin to recover the stolen ball.

The basket was open. Colin did not shoot.

The next thing Stan saw were dark, elliptical lines as something heavy and orange smashed into his face. He felt Colin's hands wrap around his throat, choking him with all his strength. Both boys tumbled to the blacktop.

Schoolyard fights at West Valley High tended to be short affairs, the combatants generally separated before too much damage could be done. However, Colin's berserk attack on Stan was so violent and so unprecedented that Cooper, Eddie, and Stan's friends could only watch in disbelief. Stan tried and failed to escape, his face turning a progressively deeper shade of purple as Colin made hoarse, barking noises in his throat.

Then Mr. Turrentine appeared between them.

---

16 "Pressure points" were often used for control moves in some forms of *ju-jitsu*, a martial art that enjoyed wide popularity among the boys of the San Fernando Valley. This was in part because of its use in mixed martial arts, but even more for its romanticized association with ninjas, mysterious Japanese assassins renowned for their ability to strike quickly and melt back into the shadows. Colin thought it would be cool to become a ninja, except for all the touching.

Later, witnesses to the event were uncertain where he had come from, or how he had moved with such speed, but there he was, pulling Colin bodily away. Stan was choking, his face bleeding, his neck bruised in the shape of Colin's grasping fingers. Mr. Turrentine tucked the barking, flailing Colin under his arm like a football and carried him off without a word.

Silence settled over the blacktop.

Cooper turned to Eddie. "Man," he said, "do *not* foul Shortbus."

Colin sat in the outer lobby of the school principal's office for nearly an hour while Dr. Doran spoke to Mr. Turrentine. They learned from Cooper that Stan had in many ways provoked the attack, which led to several calls with the school district's attorneys. They in turn had advised Dr. Doran of the possible legal consequences of punishing a special-needs student, who, it could be argued, shouldn't have been put in such a situation to begin with.

When it was all over, Dr. Doran silently handed Colin a one-day detention slip, which he accepted without complaint.

As someone who valued rules and order, Colin understood that breaking them had to come with consequences. More problematic were the stares and whispers directed his way as he walked across the cafeteria later that day. In high school, like prison, one day tended to be very much like the next. It was only natural that a disruption as unusual as Colin's would become the main topic of conversation.

Colin dealt with the attention the way he did with every stressful situation—he rededicated himself to his routine. He sat in his usual seat, spread out the neat plastic bags containing his lunch (five slices of reduced-fat salami, an apple, pretzels, celery and carrots, two Oreo cookies), and watched everyone else.

In his corner of the room, Rudy presided over his court of friends and followers, laughing while he told a story that involved miming a choking movement with his hands.

At the jocks' table, Stan sat with a Lakers hoodie zipped up high to conceal the bruises around his neck. He swallowed his sandwich slowly and carefully, occasionally swiveling his head to shoot Colin a murderous look. Cooper avoided looking at Colin at all, indicating that he either did not see Colin or did not care to. Either way, an attempt to make good on the promised interview at this time seemed ill-advised.

Colin carefully put his lunch items back into their bag, then moved toward Melissa's table. As he approached, Melissa's friends stopped their conversations. They each shot him with silent, HOSTILE stares. Melissa didn't share her friends' hostility, but she did seem uncharacteristically WARY.

"Hello, Melissa," Colin said. "How are you today?"

A silent, awkward moment followed, as Melissa debated whether to acknowledge Colin in front of her friends. Other conversations, too, trailed off. It seemed as though everyone across the entire cafeteria was watching them now.

"I'm fine, Colin. Is there something you need?"

Muffled titters erupted from the rest of Melissa's table. Colin ignored them.

"Actually, yes, there is," he continued. "Can I ask you a question?"

"Wait. I have a question for you first," Sandy declared. Her friends covered their mouths. Colin wondered if they had food stuck in their teeth and were trying to disguise it. "We hear you totally hulked out in first period PE and started whaling on Stan Krantz like he stole your pocket protector or something. True or false?"

Abby and Emma laughed aloud, confirming Colin's suspicion that Sandy's question had been rhetorical rather than literal. Melissa looked away from him. Her face flushed red from her delicately pointed chin to the tips of her ears. *EMBARRASSED.*

"I don't have a pocket protector," Colin replied. "Also, there is no pocket on my gym shirt. It's a T-shirt, and it's from Caltech. I like it much better than the one I wore yesterday because it's one hundred percent cotton and not polyester, which is a synthetic fiber. I don't like synthetic fibers because they're scratchy."

Abby and Emma laughed even louder.

"That's true. Also, if synthetic fabrics ever catch fire—"

"*Colin*," Melissa cut him off. This was also an uncharacteristic behavior. Melissa was usually very considerate about letting Colin finish his thoughts, regardless of the odd directions they would sometimes take. "Ask your question."

"If I wanted to lie to my parents, what would be the best way?"

In seventh grade, Colin noticed an unusual phenomenon. Melissa would arrive at school in long skirts or sensible, dark trousers, then disappear into the girls' room. A few minutes later, she would emerge in ripped jeans, short skirts, or whatever the popular fashion of the moment might be. At the end of the day, the process would reverse itself. Melissa always changed back into her original outfit before leaving for home.

After six months of observing this odd behavior, Colin pointed it out to Marie. He could not fathom why Melissa needed to wear two sets of clothes to school, and she refused to answer Colin's direct inquiries. Her dismissals were the closest she had ever come to demonstrating ANGER with Colin, which deterred him from pursuing it further.

"She doesn't want to wear what her parents want her to, and she doesn't want them to know," Marie had suggested to him then. The apparent deception still made very little sense to Colin, but it acceptably explained what had otherwise seemed inexplicable. It also made Melissa the ideal teacher in the art of lying.

That afternoon Colin lied to his mother for the first time.

When the call came, Mrs. Fischer was folding laundry into careful, sorted piles while leading an online teleconference with engineers from NASA facilities at JPL, Houston, Washington, DC, and Florida. "So if we drop the infrared imaging package and stagger the inspections with the final prep work, we can still make our launch window," Mrs. Fischer said, holding up a shirt and squinting to determine its owner. Her sons were getting to the age where it was becoming hard to distinguish their clothes from each other's, or her husband's. "Now—"

Her cell phone chirped. *Colin.* Mrs. Fischer paused to admire the caller ID photo—a shot of Colin emerging from the Air & Space Museum with a rare, broad smile. The image was from six years ago—half a lifetime in Colin years—but it never got old.

"One sec," she said, "the world is ending, and evidently my son is in the middle of it." There was more laughter from the group. Colin was no mystery to them; he had never been in trouble, least of all the end of the world.

Mrs. Fischer muted the conference and picked up

the phone. "I'm a little busy right now, Big C," she said. "Can this wait?"

"I'm sorry, Mom," Colin said in his usual pleasant, slightly flat tone of voice. Unlike most people, he used the exact same speech patterns for telephone and face-to-face communication. "I want to let you know I need to stay after school today. I need to do some research."

There was silence on the phone line. For an instant, his mother thought it seemed odd that Colin would be assigned a research project so early in the school year. On the other hand, Colin was prone to research projects whether they were assigned or not.

"Okay," she said. "Home by six?"

"Yes."

"See you then. Good luck with your research."

There was another, even longer silence on the line.

"Thank you," Colin said simply, and hung up.

Mrs. Fischer stared at the image of her smiling, seven-year-old son, frozen in time. Then the screen went black, and the spell was broken. And she returned to work.

Colin should have been in detention, and he knew it. This was a calculated risk, acceptable only because his window to investigate this case was already closing. Such was the nature of things. Time had a way of eroding both evidence and eyewitness memory. Colin needed both to prove Wayne Connelly was innocent.

Carefully, he placed his cell phone in his backpack

and looked down at his Notebook, oddly entranced. For the second time in less than a week, Melissa had sullied it with her feminine, cursive handwriting.

> I'm sorry, Mom. I want to let you know I need to stay after school today. I need to do some research.
> GOOD LUCK! – XO

Melissa had been sure to emphasize he was not to speak the last part aloud, but deftly avoided his question about the meaning of "XO." These were obviously not her initials, nor did they indicate a year in Roman numerals.[17] In the end, Colin circled the strange marking with a note that he should Investigate later.

Colin flipped back a page to double-check the address of his destination. He'd found himself in an unfamiliar neighborhood, and he wanted to be certain he was in the right place. He'd carefully followed the directions in his phone's map function, but Colin felt strongly that with any machine it was important not to trust, but verify.

---

17 Roman numerals (I, V, X, L, C, M) are sometimes used to designate the year, seen most often at the end of movie credits. They also often appear in the titles of major sporting events, notably the Super Bowl. For a short period during the 1980s it was even fashionable for movie sequels to use Roman numerals; e.g., *Star Trek II: The Wrath of Khan* and *Superman II*. The practice fell out of favor soon after the release of *Star Trek V: The Final Frontier* and *Superman IV: The Quest for Peace*, which may or may not have been related to their box office results, although Colin had his suspicions.

The street was lined with dingy, two-story stucco apartment buildings, crammed into the northwest corner of the San Fernando Valley. The jagged red rock formations that separated Chatsworth from Simi Valley rose up behind blocks of concrete and steel like shark's teeth flashing in the afternoon sun.

Colin walked along the cracked sidewalk, following faded addresses on the curb to the number that matched what he saw on the materials in Dr. Doran's office and copied into his Notebook. He paused to record his observations, standing vulnerable and alone before the home of Wayne Connelly.

> Wayne Connelly's house. Single story, peeling paint. Smells of cigarette smoke and stale beer. Toys scattered in the front yard, including a one-eyed doll. A hot pink Big Wheel with white tires is parked in the driveway next to a rusting Honda. Wayne is too large for the Big Wheel. Sibling?

Colin fixed on a spot of bare, faded wood beneath a peephole. A cheap buzzer had been there once, but it was gone now. It wasn't clear whether the buzzer had fallen off or been ripped out; both fates seemed equally plausible. He balled his hand into a fist to knock, suddenly remembering countless fairy tales featuring children, strange forests, and doors that should never be opened.

Colin knocked anyway.

CHAPTER EIGHT:
DUPIN'S DETACHMENT

Most casual readers think the first modern fictional detective was Sir Arthur Conan Doyle's Sherlock Holmes. This is not the case.

The origins of the modern detective story actually date half a century earlier to Edgar Allan Poe and his fictional French detective C. Auguste Dupin. In three stories—"The Purloined Letter," "The Murders in the Rue Morgue," and "The Mystery of Marie Roget"—Poe created an entirely new kind of literary crime-solver. Dupin combined a rigidly analytical mind with a vividly creative imagination and an ability to put himself in the mind-set of a deranged criminal. In the history of detective fiction, Dupin was revolutionary.

Even more revolutionary than Dupin's

techniques were his motives. Stories about heroes avenging crimes and bringing evildoers to justice go back centuries, but the emphasis had always been on the necessity of revenge, upholding personal and family honor, or the restoration of social order. Dupin was interested in none of these things.

Dupin was driven by sheer intellectual curiosity. In creating him, Poe paved the way for Holmes, Agatha Christie's Hercule Poirot, and the entire category of the gentleman detective. In so doing, he demonstrated how to reach the correct conclusion free of emotional bias or attachment to a particular outcome. What is most impressive about this accomplishment is not how quickly and easily Poe redefined the way we think about crime and punishment, but that it took so long for everybody else to catch on.

Dupin is now largely forgotten. I used to wonder why, like most modern readers, I preferred the adventures of Sherlock Holmes. It was only when reading one of my brother's Batman comics that I understood it. With his complex psychology, dark obsessions, almost inhuman energy, and intellectual gifts, Sherlock Holmes wasn't just a detective—he was the world's first superhero.

Colin smelled the inside of the house better than he could see it. Stale tobacco smoke, mildew, and the faint ammonia odor from a cat's litter box in need of changing wafted out of the darkness. A man's voice barked, "It's open!"

Colin stepped inside, carefully inhaling through his mouth and trying to pretend each aroma that caught his nostrils did not represent a microscopic particle of filth being admitted into his body. As his eyes adjusted to the darkness, he caught sight of a balding man with a wispy mustache on the sofa, his feet propped on a glass coffee table, sipping from a can of beer. On the television, a tall man with a deep Texas accent dispensed psychiatric advice to a studio audience.

"Hello, Mr. Connelly," Colin said. He tried to find something in the room that wasn't vaguely unclean so he could focus on it.

"Mr. Connelly? Good one . . ." The man's voice trailed off into a phlegmy, snorting laugh. This struck Colin as odd. His greeting hadn't been meant as a joke.

"Is Wayne at home?"

The balding man sat up straighter, his eyes narrowing at the mention of Wayne. He assessed Colin with SUSPICION. "He ain't supposed to talk to no one unless they're from the school. Did the school send you?"

"I'm from the school." Colin's face was perfectly blank. This wasn't so much a lie as being economical with the truth. It was much easier than deceiving his mother.

The man grunted. "Wayne, get your ass out here!"

he bellowed over the white noise from the television set. "Someone *from the school* wants to see you!"

A door opened somewhere in the back of the house. Heavy footsteps padded down the hallway, coming closer. Unconsciously, Colin sucked in a breath as Wayne shuffled into the living room.

"What the hell are you tal—" Wayne began to snap at the balding man, which struck Colin as a shockingly disrespectful way to address one's father. But Wayne never finished the sentence because that's when he saw Colin.

"You."

"Hello, Wayne," Colin said. "I need to talk to you."

"Outside." Wayne nodded toward the front door as he laced up a pair of cheap high-top sneakers.

The balding man swiveled his head without moving the rest of his body and caught sight of Wayne preparing to leave. He frowned. "Hey!" the man barked. "Cops said you gotta stay in the house."

"Whatever," drawled Wayne, motioning for Colin to join him in heading outside.

The balding man on the sofa wasn't ready to give up. He gestured toward an old Bakelite phone attached to the wall. "Want me to pick up the phone and call 'em?"

"Yeah, you do that, Ken," replied Wayne. "See if my mom still lets you crash here after you get her son sent back to juvie." He finished with a laugh and headed for the door. Colin laughed too. Marie had taught him that laughter was a form of social communication; in Colin's mind, he was just showing his appreciation of Wayne's joke.

Wayne clearly didn't see it the same way. He grabbed Colin roughly by the wrist and dragged him outside.

"Hey!" the balding man—*Ken*, Colin mentally noted for future reference—shouted after them. "You come back here! I swear I'll call the cops! I'm picking up the phone!" The aging screen door crashed shut, and Ken fell silent.

"Is he moving?" Wayne asked in a low voice.

"No, he's still on the sofa."

"I knew it," Wayne said. He marched Colin a short distance, then forcibly turned the much smaller boy to face him. "What the hell, Fischer? You come here to rub it in?" He balled his large hands into tight fists.

"No." Colin looked into Wayne's eyes, ignoring the reflexive aggression. It was the polite thing to do. "I came here to prove you're innocent."

Wayne stood on the sidewalk staring at Colin. He blinked seven times before he finally replied. He wasn't even trying to disguise his CONFUSION. "Come with me."

Colin followed Wayne toward a local park, past what seemed like an endless line of one-story houses with bars on the windows, badly in need of fresh paint.

Trees on the route were sparse, the sidewalks mostly in disrepair, and the cars that whizzed by seemed singularly uninterested in the safety of pedestrians. There was a faint, biting whiff of motor oil in the air. On the whole, Colin found the effect tolerable—but just barely.

The park itself was tucked up against the edge of the Santa Susana Mountains that separated the San Fernando Valley from Simi Valley to the west. "I know where we're going," Colin said. "But they've closed the park down. The officials say it's from lead contamination. There used to be skeet shooting here. But my father says that in the 1950s they tested nuclear rockets in the facility nearby, and it made the soil radioactive. Which is too bad, since they never ended up building the nuclear rockets."

Colin had long been fascinated by the huge field lab tucked away in the hills behind his neighborhood. Owned and operated by a large defense contractor, during the Cold War the facility had been home to several small experimental nuclear reactors intended to power America's space program. When he was eleven, Colin had packed three bottles of water and two energy bars and set off to investigate the site himself. Two hours later, Mr. Fischer received a call from the facility's guard shack, informing him that his son was in custody. However, by the time his father arrived, Colin's insatiable curiosity about the history of the space program had led to an unofficial tour of the grounds from the lab's director of engineering.[18]

Wayne looked over his shoulder at Colin, who couldn't read the expression at all. It appeared to be halfway between AMUSEMENT and EXASPERATION.

Wayne silently gestured to a hole that had been cut into the chain-link fence surrounding the park. Beyond it lay a green expanse of lawn, dotted with clusters of reddish-brown boulders that reminded Colin of photos of east Africa's Serengeti Plain.

"This way." Wayne pointed, leading Colin to a part of the park that couldn't be seen from the road.

"I like this park," said Colin as the two boys found a large, flat boulder on which to sit. "But it would be better if there were lions."

If Wayne had an opinion on the relative value of lions, he didn't share it. Instead, he simply said, "Talk."

So Colin did.

It took Colin less than five minutes to lay out his case: why it made no sense for Wayne to have brought the gun to school and why he believed the school authorities and law enforcement had singled Wayne out. As Colin explained it all, he carefully watched Wayne's

---

18 A little-known outpost of the Space Race of the 1960s, the Santa Susana Field Laboratory was the site of rocket-engine tests and experimental nuclear reactors. In 1959, an experimental reactor suffered the world's first nuclear meltdown, a fact known by few of the homeowners in the immediate area.

body language, how the boy went from crossing his muscular arms across his chest to drumming them against the boulder. He leaned forward to listen with growing INTEREST, flashes of INDIGNATION, and occasional ambiguously directed ANGER.

"At this point the police have nothing but suspicion based on past behavior," Colin finished. "If they had any real evidence, they'd have arrested you by now."

"When they took me in, they did one of those gunpowder tests," said Wayne, furrowing his brow and looking off to his upper right, as people often did when they tried to access their memories. "They said it came back positive."

"Anyone within fifteen feet of that gun when it went off would test positive for GSR," Colin insisted.[19] "They were trying to trick you into confessing. It's a classic interrogation technique."

"You know a lot about this stuff. Your dad a cop or something?"

"No, I just like mysteries."

Wayne looked down at his own hands before looking

---

19 GSR, or "gunshot residue," is the burnt and unburnt particles left on the skin and clothes of a shooter and his weapon, and the victim if the gun is discharged at close range. It can also be detected on the persons of nearby witnesses. Forensic scientists can use GSR to positively confirm someone's presence at a crime scene, where they were standing, or even if they fired a particular gun. It is not a perfect analytical tool because sometimes particles from other sources so closely resemble the GSR that they confuse the results.

back at Colin. "I've been kicking your ass since first grade, and now you want to clear my good name? You think if you help me, I'll leave you alone?"

"I think if I help you, I will solve the mystery."

Wayne stared at Colin for approximately fourteen seconds. Colin thought it would be rude to look at his watch, so he timed the interval by counting his heartbeats instead. Then Wayne laughed. This time, Colin decided to let him laugh alone.

"Fair enough, dude."

Colin didn't quite understand what was fair or not fair about it. It was an objective fact—although he knew that many people had trouble discerning facts from a point of view. "What other questions did the police ask you?"

"The cops kept asking me about *La Familia*."

Colin furrowed his brow, remembering the spider-web tattoo on the police detective's neck and a series of articles Colin had read in the local section of the *Los Angeles Times*. His father kept suggesting that the family cut the subscription to save money and get their news from the Internet, but Colin enjoyed the tactile sensation of reading a physical newspaper. It somehow made the news feel real. "That's a Latino gang based in the North Valley," Colin recalled.

"Very good, *vato*," Wayne said, using the East Los Angeles Chicano slang term for "man" or "homeboy," despite the fact that Wayne didn't appear to be Chicano and Colin wasn't a homeboy. "They said the gun was used in a drive-by last year in Van Nuys. Kept asking me if I run with those guys."

"Do you?" Colin asked. He tried to get a better look at Wayne's neck. Was that a tattoo or a mole?

"Oh yeah, *ese*. Blood in, blood out." Wayne affected an exaggerated Spanish accent. He turned his head just enough to reveal the mole. "*Viva la raza!*"

Colin processed this new information and created a new Notebook entry.

> Wayne Connelly—sandy hair, pale skin. <u>Claims</u>
> <u>to be Mexican</u>. Features have precedent, but
> surname is more problematic. Investigate.

He had always assumed Wayne was of Anglo-Celtic ancestry. Perhaps Wayne was mixed race, or one of his ancestors was a San Patricio soldier.[20] As he prepared to ask a follow-up question about Wayne's Latino brethren, Wayne snorted loudly. "What are you, stupid?"

"No," Colin replied. "I just have a hard time knowing when people are joking."

---

20   The San Patricio Battalions were American deserters of Irish Catholic descent, who fought on the side of Santa Ana in the Mexican-American War. They served with distinction and were considered elite artillery units. During their final losing engagements, however, they refused to surrender for fear of being punished as traitors and went so far as to shoot Mexican regulars who attempted to lay down arms. Their motives are generally ascribed to religious sympathy with fellow Catholics against a largely Protestant US Army.

"Well, I don't. I know those dudes. Drugs, guns, dog fighting—and then there's the bad stuff."

Wayne knows "those dudes." Implied familiarity. Underworld connections?

Colin nodded, knowing very well what "the bad stuff" was from the articles he'd read. "Is that why you left school on the first day? To meet with them?" This was pure conjecture on Colin's part, what television detectives might call a *fishing expedition*. It was not his preferred investigative technique, but it sometimes produced useful results.

"You ask a lot of questions," Wayne said.

"Yes."

"No." Wayne's answer was short and declarative. His expression was blank. Wayne was either telling the truth or he was a gifted liar. Either way, he had nothing more to say on the subject. Colin knew he would have to accept Wayne's denial—his metaphorical fishing expedition had landed a boot.

He was deep into planning the next step of his investigation when it occurred to him that he should share his plans with Wayne. "We know what we have to do next."

"Bend over?" Wayne interjected. He looked BITTER.

Colin raised an eyebrow. It was a gesture he'd learned from Mr. Spock, perfected through hours of practice in front of a mirror. In this case, it meant he was unable to see the utility of bending over now, or why Wayne would even consider it. "No," he said as though he had given Wayne's suggestion its due. "We find out who bought the gun and trace it to someone who was in the cafeteria when the shooting took place. The police asked me about gang activity at West Valley too, which suggests someone at school has at least some connection to *La Familia* or knows how to contact them."

"Is that all?"

Colin was busy fishing through his backpack for a map of the San Fernando Valley's bus routes, so he didn't see the look on Wayne's face and the sarcasm written there. A shame in some respects because it was the closest anyone's expression had ever come to matching Colin's cheat sheet exactly.

"It's not," Colin said as he produced the map. "Do you know where we can find a *La Familia* gun dealer?"

Wayne wondered if he was the one having a hard time understanding a joke now. He became convinced of it when Colin broke into a wide smile and pointed behind him, apropos of nothing.

"Look!" Colin exclaimed. His voice was infused with pure joy.

Wayne looked. A dun-colored coyote loped confidently along the edge of the park, toward the hills to the west. The coyote seemed to sense the boys' stares and cast an acknowledging glance at them over his shoulder. Then, as if deciding Wayne and Colin were no threat, it continued on its way.

"You're right," Wayne said with a frown, watching the coyote disappear into the brush alone. "It would be better if it were a lion."

Colin shrugged. Coyotes were pretty great too.

Fifteen minutes later, the phone rang in the Fischer kitchen. Colin's mother unloaded groceries while Danny stood in front of the open refrigerator, dissatisfied with the snacking possibilities it presented.

It was Colin. Mrs. Fischer set down a box of cereal and picked up the phone. "Hey, you. Everything okay?"

"Oh, yes," she heard Colin say. "I just realized that I need to do more research and wanted to let you know. But I should be home by dinner."

"Okay . . ." Mrs. Fischer started, trailing off as she detected an odd noise in the background of the call. It sounded like the deep hum of a diesel motor.

"Colin—is that an engine?"

"The book I need isn't at the Chatsworth Library," Colin said, as though his mother's question were never asked. "So I'm taking the bus to the Northridge branch. It shouldn't take me long."

His mother frowned. Something in the content and delivery of Colin's answer rubbed her the wrong way. Were he any other boy, Mrs. Fischer would have thought the answer sounded rehearsed, as if he had expected her to ask the question and had already prepared his reply. But Colin wasn't any other boy.

"Well . . . be careful," she finally said. "And remember, it's pizza night."

For a long moment, the only response was the distant hum of a diesel engine.

"I love you, Mom," Colin said, and hung up.

Mrs. Fischer replaced the phone in its cradle, her hand hovering above it for a moment as she debated whether or not to call Colin back. She, her husband, and a team of therapists had worked years to get Colin to the point where he could express affection for his mother without prompting. For him just to blurt it out was odd.

The first time Colin told his mother he loved her, she had just suffered through a particularly difficult day at work. She sat at the kitchen table with a bowl of ice cream (a sure sign she was in need of a morale boost) as Colin swept in from the backyard. He pounded up the stairs to his room without a word, but stopped halfway—no one knew why—and ran back to her. "I love you, Mom," he said. It was better than ice cream.

In his Notebook that night, Colin wrote:

> Today I told my mother "I love you." I am not
> sure if this was correct because she cried and

threw away her ice cream. Dad says women do
that when they are "overwhelmed," but I do not
understand what is overwhelming about a fact my
mother already knows. Investigate.

"He is so lying to you," Danny said. He slammed the refrigerator door shut and moved to the cupboard.

"Don't be silly," she replied a little too quickly. "Colin doesn't lie."

"Yeah, right." Danny stomped out to the living room with a pack of string cheese and an apple, leaving his mother alone, the groceries still unpacked.

"The library?" Wayne repeated. "That had to be the weakest story ever. How did you get her to fall for it?"

They were four miles from Colin's house now, aboard a grimy orange MTA bus, one among a fleet cruising the wide, twenty-mile-long streets that connected the San Fernando Valley from west to east. Colin rode with arms and legs pulled tight against his body. He was surrounded by strangers and presumably unfriendly faces, all packed into a space designed to comfortably carry far fewer passengers than the maximum allowed by law. It smelled strange too—acrid and sickly sweet, somewhere between the school locker room and a gas oven, now that the MTA had switched entirely to alternative fuels.

It was a near miracle that Colin had managed to

board the bus at all. Only the fact that Wayne was behind him, gently urging him forward, got Colin inside. "It's like the Mos Eisley Cantina in here," Wayne had noted as they took their seats.[21] Colin was too busy counting and thinking about the call he had to make to agree or not.

Now, Colin checked the battery level on his cell phone as he returned it to its place in his backpack. He tried not to think about the incidental contact with Wayne that resulted from shifting his belongings around. Colin looked up and saw his reflection staring back at him from the tinted glass of the bus window. His expression was blank.

"I think it was the Kuleshov Effect," Colin said. He looked down at the scrawl in his Notebook, more uneven than usual from the bumpy bus ride.

> I just realized that I need to do more research, and I wanted to let you know. (SHE WILL ASK A QUESTION, OR EXPRESS CONCERN.) The book I need isn't at the Chatsworth Library, so I'm taking

---

21 The Mos Eisley Cantina was the famous bar from the original *Star Wars* film, in which Luke Skywalker and Obi Wan Kenobi first met Han Solo. Colin puzzled at people who referred to the film as "Episode IV" or "A New Hope," since it was clearly the first movie in the series, and "Star Wars" was bombastically presented in the main titles. He also didn't understand the argument over whether Han Solo or Greedo shot first, since Greedo never actually shot anyone at all.

the bus to Northridge branch. It shouldn't take long.

"The what?"

"I kept a blank voice when I lied. And because the only context my mother has is me telling her the truth, she chose to believe me."

"You mean you never lied to her before."

The interior of the bus darkened as it passed beneath the huge concrete expanse of the 405 freeway, heading east through endless miles of strip malls, bungalows, and crumbling, stucco-sided apartment buildings. The suburban wasteland stretched from Panorama City to the Verdugo Mountains. Colin watched it pass by through the blue-gray tint of the bus window, thinking about the coyote, and how coyotes had been here since this was all just rocks and trees and grass.

"Yes," Colin said, realizing he had just crossed a Rubicon.[22] "It was . . . *easy*."

---

22 The Rubicon is a river in Italy, famed for Julius Caesar's crossing in 49 BC. Because Caesar's action plunged the Roman Empire into war, the phrase "crossing the Rubicon" is meant to suggest a point of no return. Ironically, the shifting course of the Rubicon makes it impossible to determine where the real, historical "point of no return" actually lies.

CHAPTER NINE:
THE PARKING PROBLEM

Life is math.

We know this because mathematicians can reduce anything to a system of equations. Sometimes, the solutions tell us things that seem "intuitively obvious." This means that we do not need math to figure them out. For example, the Parking Problem.

Some mathematicians at a university wanted to know how people could minimize the time it takes to find a parking spot and get into a store. Here is what they found: The optimal strategy is to take the first space you see and then walk.

When I told my father about this, he asked why it took mathematicians at a university to figure it out. I explained that while the conclusion seems intuitively obvious, it runs counter to standard human

> behavior. Most people will not take the first space
> they come across. Instead, they will seek out a better,
> theoretical spot that could be more convenient,
> incorrectly believing it will save them time.
>
> I used to think people did this because they're
> bad at math, but actually it's because they're
> gamblers. They pass up good opportunities that are
> right in front of them in exchange for imagined
> improvements that almost never materialize. This
> is why I trust math and I do not trust people. Math
> makes better decisions.

Colin and Wayne stood on the walk outside a stucco
box of a house with a weed-choked lawn and a heavily
fenced-in backyard that had never seen a clump of sod.
Two pit bulls snarled and hurled themselves against the
sturdy wire mesh with an angry, metallic rattle. Their
job was to deter visitors, and for the most part, they
did it well. Colin didn't see danger; he merely stared
back at the would-be monsters, cocking his head to one
side. The dogs licked their lips, sighed, and sat back on
their haunches.

"How the hell did you do that?" Wayne asked,
IMPRESSED.

Colin shrugged.

"Whatever," Wayne said. He pointed at the house.
"Here's the profile: I've dealt with these guys before, so
let me take the lead here."

"Okay," Colin said, writing this down.

"Don't mention the cops or the school investigation."

Colin nodded, writing this down too.

"And if they ask you questions, just be cool."

"Cool," Colin repeated. He wrote *I'm cool* in his Notebook.

"And put your Notebook away. Don't let them see that."

Colin considered this a moment, then stuffed his Notebook in his backpack. He would have to record the particulars of the experience later from memory.

"You know what?" Wayne said finally. "Just don't say anything."

Wayne took a step in front of Colin and drew a deep breath, then started up the walk. Colin followed, silent as a mouse. Wayne rapped on the front door.

For a moment, it seemed like no one was going to answer. Then the door swung open, answered by a boy who couldn't have been older than ten. The boy looked at them.

"Hello," Colin said.

Wayne shot him a withering look, but didn't touch him. Colin fell silent, making a mental note to put aside his usual social scripts. Wayne turned back to the boy at the door, taking charge. "We're here to see *El Cocodrilo*," he declared.

Colin tried not to betray his surprise at Wayne's use of the name. If Wayne knew who this *El Cocodrilo* person was, he hadn't mentioned him before. Colin resisted the impulse to search his Notebook for an earlier reference—successful mainly because he knew there could be none. What else was Wayne not telling him? Colin was determined to investigate the matter later. For now, the danger before him was more than enough.

The boy didn't answer. Instead, he turned back inside, leaving the door open. It was a non-answer and an invitation, all in one. Colin was impressed with his efficiency.

Wayne and Colin followed the boy into the house.

Colin's nose twitched, detecting chicken, ham, and cheese cooking together. It smelled good, a welcome and comforting surprise. He occupied himself by wondering what could be on the stove as they passed through the living room. On the television, someone— probably the boy, Colin imagined—had paused a first-person shooter video game with something that looked like an alien or a demon caught in the crosshairs of a rocket-powered grenade launcher.

In the kitchen, three monstrous *vatos* with half-consumed beers watched them enter. The *vatos'* expressions changed rapidly at the sight of them, from CON-CERNED to CONFUSED to . . . well, Colin wasn't sure, but it looked a little like AMUSED. There was laughter, a few words in Spanish that Colin couldn't understand, and then they went back to drinking their beers. Colin surmised they were *La Familia*.

A tall, lanky man in his early twenties worked the stove, making what Colin now knew to be chicken cordon bleu. "If you're selling magazines," he said, "I get it cheaper at the newsstand."

"Wow," replied Wayne with a genuine enthusiasm that led Colin to conclude that he didn't smell many expertly prepared meals in his own home, "that smells really good."

"Yeah, but it's coming out dry." The lanky man frowned at his pan.

"You should turn it down to simmer," Colin offered helpfully, "and cover it the last five minutes."

Wayne looked at Colin again. His *PAINED* expression was lost on Colin, but it was enough to remind him of his promise to remain silent. The lanky man looked at him too, considering his advice. Then he opened his huge mouth to laugh, revealing rows of perfect white teeth. He turned down the stove and covered his pan as Colin suggested.

"*El Cocodrilo,*" Colin guessed aloud, unable to help himself.

"The very one, *ese,*" *El Cocodrilo* said. "So what's your name, L'il Emeril?"

It suddenly occurred to Colin that offering his real name could be a strategic mistake. This was an undercover investigation, which classically required an alias. Colin decided to provide one. Lying was getting easier all the time.

"Tommy Westphall," Colin said, trying very hard to keep a blank expression.

"You boys are a long way from Tarzana."

"Chatsworth," Wayne corrected. The last thing he needed was for *El Cocodrilo* to get caught up in a geography lesson, courtesy of Colin Fischer. "We heard this was the place to come if we want *something*."

"*Something*, huh? Who says?"

"A friend," Wayne answered.

"Which friend?"

"A *good* friend."

El Cocodrilo stared Wayne down in what Colin recognized as pure animal assertion of dominance. Wayne refused to show submission, instead asserting himself as a social equal to the gang leader by meeting *El Cocodrilo's* gaze and staring back at him evenly. A risky strategy, Colin surmised, unless Wayne believed he could back it up—or he simply didn't care if he could or not. It was impossible to say. In the end, it was *El Cocodrilo* who looked away first. He shook his head in DISGUST, though it didn't seem directed at Wayne. He turned to his *vatos*. "As soon as I saw the fool and that gap-toothed freak friend of his, I knew he'd shoot his mouth off," he lamented.

"Truth," one of the *vatos* said.

Colin realized immediately whom *El Cocodrilo* was talking about. The only "gap-toothed freak" he knew was Stan. Which strongly suggested "the fool" was—

137

"Eddie," Wayne said, having figured it out on his own. Colin was impressed with Wayne's unanticipated and welcome display of deductive powers. Wayne had now managed to catch Colin off guard three times in less than ten minutes. It was quite a feat.

El Cocodrilo shrugged at Wayne, as if to confirm his suspicions without ever going on record with a name. "Said he had someone he wanted to show *it* to. Was gonna make him piss his pants." The way *El Cocodrilo* said *it*, Colin understood that he was consciously avoiding the word *gun*.

"You know Eddie," Wayne pressed. "I asked him to loan it to me, but he wouldn't. Told me to get my own." Wayne's response was so effortless that Colin was suddenly confronted with the possibility that Wayne had been telling him the truth, but was also a gifted liar. In a way, it made him more credible.

"That what you're here for, *ese*? Your own?"

Colin recognized this as what his father called "put up or shut up" time.[23] Either they would need to explain their purpose here (put up) or *El Cocodrilo* planned to show them the door (shut up). Wayne never

---

23 The precise origin of the phrase is in question, but Colin understood it in the context of learning to play poker. "Put up" meant to meet the call, and "shut up" meant to fold. An avid Texas Hold 'Em player, Mr. Fischer was less than delighted to discover that Colin's uncanny memory and lack of emotional indicators made it impossible to tell when he was bluffing. "I have to take you to Vegas someday," Mr. Fischer would say. What he really meant was "I'd rather play against your mother."

got the chance to choose either. The sound of gunshots and explosions suddenly blasted through the house. Reflexively, everyone in the kitchen froze and turned toward the source.

It was the boy, finishing his video game in the living room.

For everyone but Colin, this was a relief. The others chuckled and otherwise assumed relaxed postures, thinking the threat had passed, but Colin could feel his heart thumping in his chest. He covered his ears with his hands, breathing hard. "No noise, no noise, no noise . . . !"

One of the *vatos* pointed at Colin with his beer. "'Sup with Tommy?"

"It's nothing. He just gets this way sometimes. Funny, right?" Wayne smiled like it was a joke. Like it was nothing. *El Cocodrilo* and his boys weren't laughing.

"No noise, no noise, no noise . . . !" Colin didn't stop.

Wayne shifted uncomfortably. He had no idea how to make Colin stop, or even why he had started. He only knew that the air had become tense and confused as a result and that tension, confusion, and gangbangers with weapons were a bad combination.

"There is definitely something wrong with that kid," *El Cocodrilo* said. He turned down his stove. The *vatos* stood up as Colin's shouts became high-pitched yelps.

In the yard, the dogs started barking again.

"Colin!" Wayne snapped.

It only took Wayne a moment to realize his mistake, but in that moment, everything changed. The boy in the living room paused his video game. The room fell silent. Colin stopped yelping and tried to compose himself. His breathing returned to normal as he took note of the expression on *El Cocodrilo*'s face: SUSPICIOUS.

"That was inappropriate, and I'm really very sorry for doing that," Colin said, hoping that would be enough to defuse any potential awkwardness. It wasn't.

"Sure you are, *Tommy Westphall*," *El Cocodrilo* said with a frown. The gangbangers moved closer, slowly surrounding Colin and Wayne. "Or *Colin*. Or whoever, man."

Wayne made a snap decision. "Run!"

He grabbed Colin by the arm and hauled him out of the kitchen through the living room. Colin could barely process what was happening now. He was caught between understanding the need to flee from *El Cocodrilo* and irrational horror at Wayne's touch.

"Please don't touch me!" Colin cried.

"Shut up!"

A split second later, Colin and Wayne sprinted out the front door to safety.

Colin and Wayne ran down an unfamiliar street.

As they raced by an endless parade of strip malls,

Colin remembered what it was like to be six years old and running for his life across the playground. He remembered the slides and the swing sets and the monkey bars, passing in a blur. He remembered the pressure in his chest, the taste of blood and his own salty tears, the dull pain in his lip. He remembered how hard it was to breathe and scream, to urge his body forward as fast it would go. In his mind, Colin could still see the faces of the other children, who weren't sure what to make of his terror. Some laughed and pointed, like chimpanzees in a zoo. Chattering. Then as now, he feared for his life. Then as now, Wayne Connelly ran behind him.

That night when he was six, Colin made the following entry in his Notebook:

> Today I learned how to run very fast.

Only now, Wayne had probably just saved his life. This was yet another unexpected turn in a day full of unexpected turns, and yet another surprise from Wayne Connelly. Colin wished he had time to pause and record his thoughts, but that time would have to come later.

El Cocodrilo and *La Familia* were close behind. This was worrisome. However, the *vatos* were older, slower, and (from the distribution of weight on their bodies) clearly not used to running long distances.

Also, they smelled like cigarettes, particularly *El Cocodrilo*. Colin calculated that he and Wayne had a reasonable chance of escape if they just kept running straight.

Wayne clearly didn't agree with Colin's assessment. He veered off sharply into a Vons grocery store parking lot. Colin followed him. There was no time to argue.

The lot was very busy. A car horn blared in Colin's ears, and he realized that he and Wayne had barely avoided being run over. Colin covered his ears as the boys zigged and zagged through the rows of parked cars, occasionally doubling back. This had the effect of sowing confusion among *La Familia*, who split up to cut them off.

Wayne and Colin sprinted for the grocery store entrance, past a security guard who looked SURPRISED to see two boys blow by with an angry gang in hot pursuit.

As they skidded into the produce section and took cover behind a banana stand, they watched the security guard step in front of *El Cocodrilo* and the others. Colin couldn't hear what they were saying, although the security guard's hand on his radio told him it probably involved a call to the police. The *vatos* strained to see their prey over the racks of fruits and vegetables as the guard shooed them out, but they'd been stymied.

Wayne and Colin took a second to catch their breath. "Where the hell did you learn to run like that?"

Wayne asked, hands on his knees and sucking down oxygen.

"First grade," Colin said. "After that time you beat me up next to the swing set."

Wayne considered Colin for what seemed to Colin like a very long time, his expression frozen. Colin was confused. All he had done was provide a factual answer to Wayne's question. Colin wondered if he'd said something wrong without realizing it. This occurred often, so it wouldn't have surprised Colin at all if he had.

Finally, Wayne looked away. "Oh," he said.

Mr. Fischer answered the phone on the third ring.

"Hello, Dad. This is Colin."

"Colin?" Mr. Fischer asked with feigned confusion. "Colin who?"

"Your son," Colin explained helpfully.

"Oh, *that* Colin," Mr. Fischer replied. "I almost forgot I had a son named Colin because he missed dinner."

"I missed dinner because I'm at the Vons grocery store in Sylmar. And I have no money for a bus, and I need a ride home."

"Sylmar," Mr. Fischer repeated, enunciating the word carefully to make certain he'd heard Colin correctly. He looked at his wife, who had just entered the living room. "It's Colin," he explained, covering the receiver, "He's in Sylmar."

"*Sylmar?* Holy sh—!"

"Shhh." Mr. Fischer said, holding a finger to his lips. Mrs. Fischer pursed her own lips as tight as she could, a little afraid herself of what might come out.

"Dad?" Colin asked through the phone.

"Yes, son. I'm here."

Mrs. Fischer gave her husband the MOM FACE, the one that demanded to be told what was going on. He waved her off. He didn't really know what was going on, and he suspected getting Colin to tell him anything substantial would take some effort.

"My friend Wayne needs a ride too."

"Wayne . . . Connelly?" Mr. Fischer guessed, trying to mask his concern. This was as much for his wife's benefit as Colin's. He knew that nothing was more dangerous and unpredictable than a mother who believed her child was in distress.

"*Wayne Connelly?*" Mrs. Fischer exclaimed. "Holy sh—!"

"Shhh!" Mr. Fischer turned away from her, shielding the phone with his body.

"Oh, I hate you," she declared. He blew her a kiss over his shoulder.

"Yes," Colin finally said. "Wayne Connelly. Can you give him a ride?"

"Of course," his father said. "I'm coming, Colin. Just sit tight."

"Thank you."

There was a brief silence before Colin spoke again. "Dad?"

"Yes, son."

"You should look for a parking spot very close to the door. As close as you can get—even if it takes you more time." Then there was silence at the other end of the line. Colin had hung up, having said everything he'd intended to say.

Danny loped into the room. "Was that the spaz?" he asked.

"Your brother is in Sylmar with Wayne Connelly," Mr. Fischer explained.

"Don't call him *the spaz*," Mrs. Fischer warned.

"Sylmar. Not the library?" A broad smile spread across Danny's face. He burst into triumphant laughter, which ended with a light smack to the back of his head.

"Say it," his mother warned, "and I'll end all of your troubles forever."

Danny made a face, but he knew well enough to keep any further I-told-you-so to himself. He wandered back to the kitchen in a funk. Even a moment of vindication could be stymied by his brother's weirdness.

Mr. Fischer grabbed his wallet and keys and headed for the door.

"I'm coming with you," Mrs. Fischer said.

Mr. Fischer held up a hand and shook his head. "Let me explain something about boys," he began.

"Sometimes, the last thing in the world a boy wants is his mother—especially when he needs her the most."

"That's stupid."

"Yes."

With that, Mr. Fischer set out alone into the night to rescue his boy.

Colin stared at his cell phone a moment before stuffing it into his backpack. Something about his father's tone confused him, but he couldn't quite identify it. He wondered about the loud sounds from his mother and the laughter from his brother. Did his family know he'd lied? Either way, Colin knew he'd find out soon enough.

"Well?" Wayne asked behind him.

"My father is coming to get us."

For a moment, Wayne's face froze. He turned away from Colin, perhaps realizing that his uneasy ally was trying to read his expression. "Great," Wayne muttered.

"Yes."

Then, thinking nothing more of it, Colin produced his Notebook and a green-ink pen and began to write.

CHAPTER TEN:
ROGUE PREDATORS

The Serengeti Plains are home to the greatest variety and concentration of megafauna on planet Earth.

How do so many different animals manage to share one geographic space? By specializing. Each species occupies its own niche in the Serengeti ecosystem. In a place where the different species have to come together—for example, a watering hole—the animals avoid conflict by moving in predictable patterns. Even the carnivores drink at set times, allowing their prey to plan accordingly.

However, every ecosystem has its rogue predators, the most dangerous animals of all. Because they don't follow any patterns, their behavior can't be predicted or planned for. You never know when one will show up at the watering hole to cause trouble.

In the short term, rogue behavior is an excellent survival strategy. The unpredictability increases the chances that potential prey will find itself out in the open and vulnerable. In the long term, the strategy can't sustain itself. The system adapts. Would-be midnight snacks fall back even more on the protection of the herd, making food harder to come by. Other predators are affected by this and react with displeasure to an interloper who doesn't follow the rules.

Usually, the rogue comes to an unhappy end. Though sometimes, the responses from the environment force a change in its behavior, resulting in a sort of rehabilitation. I find it interesting that in this respect, the animal kingdom isn't much different from human civilization—in the end, crime doesn't pay. And punishment can have results as varied as the species of the Serengeti Plains.

Wayne wandered back toward the magazine section, where Colin sat writing. "They're still there," he announced. "I think they're trying to wait us out."

Colin nodded, not really paying attention. He was too focused on recording his thoughts on everything that happened since Wayne instructed him to put his Notebook away. He had many.

"Did you hear me?" Wayne asked.

Colin blinked at him behind his glasses. "Yes," he replied. "They're still there. You think they're trying to wait us out." He went back to writing.

Wayne stared at Colin with a CURIOUS frown, trying to make sense of this weird kid. It was impossible. So he did the only thing he could do—he grabbed a car magazine to pass the time while they awaited rescue. He flipped through it, mainly looking at pictures of the sports cars he desperately wanted to drive someday when he had a license.

"What's in that Notebook, anyway?" Wayne asked, reading.

"Facts," Colin answered, still writing.

"Facts about what?"

"Facts about everything."

"Oh."

Wayne opened to a photo of a new Porsche 911 and smiled. "Porsche," he said. "My dad had one of these. My real dad." Wayne closed the magazine with a frown and jammed it back into the rack a little too hard, crinkling the binding.

"You have a real dad?" Colin asked.

"Yeah." Wayne reached for another magazine. Out of the corner of his eye, he saw Colin was still writing. "Are you writing that down?"

"Yes."

"I thought you said it was all facts."

"It is. And thoughts."

Wayne looked at Colin seriously. "Can I read it? Your Notebook, I mean."

"No."

There was a long silence between them. Low-grade alarm tickled Colin's chest. He was vaguely concerned that Wayne would simply take it from him. Experience told him this wasn't an unreasonable worry.

"Okay," Wayne said finally. He consumed an article about modified power trains, but only with halfhearted interest. His eyes kept drifting toward Colin and his Notebook. If Colin was aware of the attention, he gave no indication.

"Is there other stuff about me in there?" Wayne asked, trying to sound offhand.

"Oh, yes," Colin replied. "There are several entries about you. In fact, I would say that you appear in these pages more often than anyone outside my family or possibly Melissa Greer." Colin thought a moment and then added, "Melissa is my friend."

"Your friend," Wayne repeated.

"Yes," Colin said. "Melissa has always been nice to me."

"Do you, um . . . just write about nice things that people do?"

"Oh, no."

"And how long have you been writing in that thing?"

"Since preschool," Colin explained.

"Right."

Wayne put back the second magazine and slumped down next to Colin.

"Seriously, dude," he said. "What the hell is wrong with you?"

"Asperger's syndrome is a neurological condition related to—"

"Yeah, yeah," Wayne interrupted him. "I know you're like a really smart retard or something. I mean . . . *what the hell is wrong with you*? What are you doing here? Why are you trying to help me?"

"You're innocent."

"Innocent." Wayne leaned back against the rack and shook his head. "No, man. I'm not. I just didn't do it."

"Colin," a man's voice said. Colin recognized it instantly. He looked up and saw his father standing there, staring at them. He looked WORRIED.

"Hello, Dad," Colin said. "How was your day?"

"Good." Mr. Fischer narrowed his eyes, taking a moment to process the sight of his son sitting with Wayne Connelly. "Let's go home."

They were almost to Wayne's neighborhood when the silence broke. "So, Wayne," Mr. Fischer said, "you and Colin . . . you're friends. In school?"

It sounded a bit like a test, and in a sense it was. Mr. Fischer knew very well how things could change

151

between children over time, especially between boys. Conflict had a way of forging friendships, a story as old as the epic of Gilgamesh and Enkidu.[24] The friend in this case wasn't necessarily someone he would have chosen for his son, but Mr. Fischer understood the choice wasn't his to make.

"Um . . . yeah," Wayne managed.

"Wayne is the reason I came home from school early on the first day," Colin offered suddenly. "He put my head in the sink, and then he put my head in the toilet and he flushed it."

Mr. Fischer forced a smile. Wayne shifted uneasily in his seat.

"Um. Yeah," Wayne said again, hoping Colin would leave it there.

"People think he brought a gun to school, but I know he didn't because there was frosting on the gun and Wayne eats very neatly." Colin was certain that a statement of the facts would allay any concerns his father might have.

Mr. Fischer shot a look at Wayne in the rearview mirror, somewhere between a question and a warning.

---

24 Gilgamesh was the lonely and cruel king of Uruk. He first battled and then befriended the wild man called Enkidu, with whom he had had many adventures and fought the demon Humbaba. Through his unlikely friendship with the strange, unpredictable outsider, Gilgamesh grew into a good and just king and a hero. Colin had read this was how most friendships began between men—combat, followed by misadventure. It made him wonder if his aversion to wrestling was also the reason for his relative solitude.

The more he learned, he realized, the less he knew. "That's . . . fantastic," he said.

Mercifully, it wasn't long before Mr. Fischer's sedan pulled up to the curb near Wayne's house. Colin noticed someone had taken the pink Big Wheel inside as Wayne wordlessly climbed out of the car.

He was halfway to his front door when Colin's father spoke up after him. "Wayne, wait."

Wayne took a deep breath. Mr. Fischer was standing by the driver's door, looking decidedly uncomfortable with the whole situation. "If you think they wouldn't mind," Mr. Fischer began, "I'd like to talk to your parents for a minute."

Wayne looked at his shoes. "Yeah. They're not home. They go out a lot. You know, the movies."

Colin watched the exchange from the backseat. He wrinkled his nose with confusion, having never seen this particular emotion from Wayne before. Indeed, Colin had thought Wayne incapable of it. There was no recourse but to consult the cheat sheet. Colin flipped through flash cards, finally forced to accept what he could plainly see:

Wayne Connelly was AFRAID.

Mr. Fischer drummed his fingers on the hood of the car, weighing the pros and cons of marching up to the Connellys' door whether Wayne liked it or not. He didn't need permission from a fourteen-year-old boy. On the other hand, there were things he didn't know about this particular boy—and there was always the chance that a talk with Wayne's parents would do far more harm than good.

"Right," Mr. Fischer said finally. "Some other time, then." He slid back into the driver's seat and put the car into gear.

Wayne hesitated a moment, then gestured at Colin to roll down the window, which Colin did. "Mr. Fischer?" Wayne started as the barrier dropped. "Thanks. For picking us up I mean." He looked at Colin with a frown that Colin couldn't fathom at all. "And Fischer . . . *Colin*. I'm really sorry about the swing set."

With that, Wayne disappeared inside his house.

Colin and his father heard the echo of a man shouting Wayne's name and something else (unpleasant). For a moment, Mr. Fischer just sat there staring at the steering wheel. Then he turned to his son, a tight smile drawing his lips together, though Colin was quite certain his father wasn't HAPPY.

"Are you angry with me?" Colin asked, guessing.

Mr. Fischer didn't answer, which left Colin more perplexed than ever. Did his father want him to guess again? Was he too angry for words? Colin understood this was conceivable but had (to his knowledge) never actually inspired it in his parents. For the first time, Colin grappled with the possibility that he was in very serious trouble. Just as he was about to say "I'm sorry," Mr. Fischer raised a hand with his fingers splayed.

"Coming in for a landing," he said.

Colin braced himself as his father laid a hand on his shoulder and squeezed. It was a gentle squeeze, and it did not feel ANGRY or seem to have any point at all other than to be exactly what it was.

Then they drove away, and Mr. Fischer did not speak again.

PART THREE:
THE OLYMPIC TRAMPOLINE TEAM

CHAPTER ELEVEN
HELL IS OTHER PEOPLE

My father designs drive systems for unmanned spacecraft at the Jet Propulsion Laboratory in Pasadena. This sounds very exotic and futuristic, but in fact the engines my father works on are chemical rockets that would be recognizable to Goddard, von Braun, Parsons, or the other rocketry pioneers of sixty years ago.

Other methods of powering interplanetary spacecraft have been proposed over the decades, from solar sails to ion engines and nuclear pulse propulsion, which involved ejecting atomic bombs from the rear of a spacecraft and exploding them against a metal pusher plate to launch the ship to the outer planets. None of these developed to maturity, which my father regards as the major impediment to manned space travel beyond the moon.

However, the real problems lie not in mechanical limitations, but human ones.

Using chemical rockets, a manned trip to Mars would take a minimum of six months in each direction. Astronauts on such a long journey would be subjected to the long-term physical stresses of microgravity, causing their muscles to atrophy and bones to weaken. Also, cosmic rays beyond the Earth's magnetic field would bombard them with harmful radiation. (Apollo astronauts on lunar journeys reported "flashes" of light whenever they closed their eyes, as cosmic rays collided with their retinas.)

All of that is difficult to overcome, but they remain engineering problems. No engineering solution can address the psychological hurdle—the mental stresses caused by a handful of people living in close proximity for months at a time, with no hope for escape and no opportunities for solitude. "I've seen the reports from the Antarctic research stations, and they aren't pretty," my father told me. When I asked him why, he answered with a quote from a play by Jean-Paul Sartre, "No Exit": "Hell is other people."

Colin and his father found his mother and Danny waiting for them in the kitchen.

"Everything's fine," Mr. Fischer said flatly.

Danny leaned forward in his chair, letting his spoon fall into his ice cream bowl with a sharp clink. "Is he in trouble?" Danny asked, incongruously HOPEFUL. Colin was too hungry and too tired to subject his brother's reaction to more detailed analysis.

Mr. Fischer considered his sons in turn, aware of Danny's attitude but in no way sympathetic to it. "Colin, take your dinner and go to your room," he said. "Danny, how we discipline your brother isn't your problem." He was very matter-of-fact.

Colin murmured a low "thank you" as he grabbed a plate of pizza from under the glass cover that was keeping it warm and fished in the open refrigerator for water. He tested the bottles' temperatures each in turn with his hand so he could take the coldest, then quietly padded up the stairs, mentally reviewing the events of the day. There were almost too many; the best next step in the investigation felt like a warm bath and a good night's sleep.

Danny watched him go, turning back to his father when Colin was safely up the stairs, out of earshot. "So he's not in trouble," he said.

"Zip it, or you will be," Mrs. Fischer replied. Danny opened his mouth to argue, but his mother was quicker. "No comments from the peanut gallery.[25] I want every

---

25 Mrs. Fischer had learned the phrase from her own mother without having any idea what it actually meant. Eight-year-old Colin helpfully pointed out that "peanut gallery" was an old vaudeville term used to

peanut in the house in bed. Five minutes. Go." Early on, she worried the techniques she used to manage teams of engineers would bleed over and complicate her efforts to discipline her children. Now she knew that engineers and children were the same animal.

Danny trudged loudly up the stairs without another word or editorial sigh, each deliberate step registering his disapproval. A moment later, the click of his bedroom door echoed down to the kitchen. There was a soft *thud* as his small body flopped onto a bed.

The Fischer parents sat at the kitchen table, two large glasses of wine already waiting for them. Then a new sound came—water, running through the pipes upstairs.

"Colin," Mr. Fischer guessed, "taking a bath." He took a generous sip of red wine. "I can't say I blame him."

Mrs. Fischer sighed heavily. "We were hoping high school would make him more independent. Be careful what you wish for, right?"

"Independent? Independent is fine. But there's independent, and there's going rogue."

"Lying, running across town with a juvenile delinquent . . . Where does it end?" Mrs. Fischer frowned. Danny's soda bottle had etched a faint ring into the

---

describe the cheapest seats in a theater and the rowdy patrons who would sit there, jeering and tossing peanuts at performers they didn't like. Colin solemnly promised never to throw peanuts at his mother.

surface of her kitchen table. She used the end of her sleeve to rub it away.

"The cat might as well start barking for all the sense it makes," Mr. Fischer said, looking around to see where the cat had gone.

"God, no. Bad enough that he likes to curl up around my face at night."

"So what can we do about it?"

"Nothing. I throw him off; he just climbs back on. Little bastard."

Mr. Fischer playfully flicked a bottle cap from Danny's discarded soda in his wife's direction. She caught it expertly, then tossed it in a wastebasket across the sink.

"We can revisit the special-school option," she said. "But we both know . . ."

". . . that's wrong. Maybe it's easier for us. But it's wrong for him."

"There was a time when what was right for him was easier for us."

"Oh yeah? When was that?" Mr. Fischer smiled.

Water gurgled through the pipes overhead, draining from a bathtub. "Three minutes exactly," Mrs. Fischer noted. "The boy is like a machine."

"You know," Mr. Fischer said, "I'm gonna miss the days when he just wanted to stay in his room, read about sharks, and listen to *Rubber Soul* over and over again."

There was a moment of silence. The bathroom door opened upstairs.

"So not missing the *Rubber Soul*."

"Yeah, okay. Me neither." Mr. Fischer shook his head, like he was escaping some distant psychological trauma. But the floodgates had opened, now. "Or how about the listing of the scientific inaccuracies in *Jaws*. You remember when—"

He never finished his sentence. His voice was drowned out by a deafening *crash* from upstairs, followed by frantic, hysterical shouting. The Fischers sprang to their feet and raced upstairs, taking the steps in twos.

They found Colin in his pajamas before the open door to his room, screaming, not entirely coherently. A violent torrent of words exploded from him. "HE RUINED IT HE DESTROYED EVERYTHING WHY WOULD HE DO THIS EVERYTHING IS RUINED IT'S ALL WRONG HE DESTROYED IT HE RUINED EVERYTHING . . ."

Mr. Fischer approached slowly, speaking in a low, calming voice, his arms relaxed and hands open, careful not to touch Colin or even suggest that he might. This was not the first time they had seen this behavior, and it would not be the last. "Colin, buddy. What happened? Tell me what happened."

Mrs. Fischer looked beyond Colin and immediately

saw the source of anger and panic. His bed was unmade, the sheets tossed back. The carefully arranged stacks of books had fallen from their shelves, the contents of his desk lay in a pile on the floor. It was as if they had been swept there with one violent arm motion. Beneath the cork board along Colin's wall, the photographs he had so painstakingly printed, arranged, and tacked into place lay strewn like autumn leaves, strands of yarn still connecting them together.

Mrs. Fischer repeated in a reassuring tone, "Colin, don't worry. Colin, don't worry. We'll fix it." She spoke his name deliberately. It was a way of connecting with him when he was in this state. She reached out to clasp his arm—sometimes, Colin allowed her contact he would not under some circumstances allow his father—but Colin roughly twisted away from her touch. He pointed an accusing finger down the hallway.

"WHY DID YOU DO THAT WHY WOULD YOU RUIN EVERYTHING YOU RUINED EVERYTHING YOU DESTROYED IT ALL . . ."

Danny stood at the doorway to his own room. His arms were crossed over his chest and eyes downcast in an expression Colin would have recognized as DEFIANT had he been processing rationally. "What?" Danny said, more a challenge than a question.

Colin lunged toward his younger brother, screaming. "WHY DID YOU RUIN EVERYTHING?" he

165

roared as his father stepped into his path and wrapped his arms around him. Mr. Fischer gripped his son tightly, Colin's face buried in his shoulder.

It was in its own way an extreme measure. To the outside world, it might look as though he were smothering his son, but the hard, even pressure against Colin's long nerves slowly calmed him.[26] His harsh, ragged breathing began to steady and slow. It became more even. More oxygen entered Colin's system, calming him.

As Colin melted, his mother turned her attention to Danny. "What did you do?"

Danny stared at his feet, avoiding his mother's gaze. "I couldn't find my iPod," he mumbled. "I thought Colin might have taken it."

His answer undid everything his father's embrace had accomplished. "I DID NOT I NEVER TAKE YOUR THINGS I DON'T EVEN LIKE YOUR MUSIC . . ."

Mr. Fischer renewed his grip on Colin. "Colin, easy."

He struggled to ratchet down Colin's latest outburst, holding him tight as his wife marched toward

---

26 The technique was inspired by famous autistic livestock handler and author Temple Grandin, who observed that the "squeeze box" used to immobilize cattle for vaccinations and medical examinations also had the effect of calming the animals. Grandin later adapted the box into a "hug machine" of her own design that she crawled into when she was under emotional duress. As Colin grew and matured, Mr. Fischer realized that this ad hoc technique of calming his son would eventually lose its effectiveness.

Danny. The younger boy flinched, despite the fact that in his entire life, his mother had never done more than lightly swat him on the bottom. His reaction was purely instinctive. On some level, all children know their mothers are fully capable of killing and eating them. Danny was no different.

"And that gives you the right to tear apart his room?" Mrs. Fischer demanded. She knew how furious she was and was doing her damnedest not to make things worse by indulging herself. "You know how Colin is about his things being moved."

Danny reacted like any animal when cornered. He chose to fight. His yell started at the balls of his feet and ended at his forehead, the adrenaline consuming him as he let loose. "You're damn right I know how he is! You all walk on tippy-toes around him and are all 'Oh, poor Colin' whenever he acts like a retard and I'm the one who gets—"

"*What did you call him*?" There was no containing the anger now.

Danny visibly cowered against the doorframe. He had never seen his mother this angry, and he was afraid. His defiant petulance gave way to backpedaling defensiveness. In primate terms, the alpha female had bared her teeth. Now it was the juvenile's turn to show submission. "I—I didn't say he was one. I said he was *acting* like one."

Mrs. Fischer stood six inches from Danny, deep

ASHLEY EDWARD MILLER & ZACK STENTZ

inside his personal space. "We do not use that word in this house," she growled. "You especially don't use it toward your brother. You will *never* use it again. I don't care how he acts."

"You think he doesn't hear it whenever he goes out that door?" Danny asked, suddenly quiet. "Do you know the things they call him?"

"I have a pretty good idea," his mother snapped, voice rising. "Which makes it even more important he doesn't hear it from the people who are *supposed* to love him!"

Danny looked past her to Colin, squeezed into his father's shoulder. The HATE returned to his lips. "Well . . . maybe I *don't*. Maybe I *hate* him. I HATE YOU, COLIN, YOU'RE A *RETARD* AND I HATE YOU—"

"*Danny!*" Mrs. Fischer shouted. She reached for him, her hands like claws.

"Susan!" Mr. Fischer barked, trying to keep everyone together. Powerless.

"It doesn't bother me," Colin said suddenly. He was very calm.

Everyone stopped. Mrs. Fischer and Danny both turned to Colin, the unexpected voice of reason. Mr. Fischer relaxed his grip on his son, who was still red-faced but much calmer. Colin faced his mother and younger brother.

"No, really," he insisted. "Mental retardation is defined by having an IQ below 70 to 75. My IQ is . . ."

Colin stopped himself. Marie had taught him not

to discuss his actual IQ, which had been tested at any-where between 155 and 180.[27] She told him it would sound to others like he was bragging. ". . . higher than that," Colin finished. "Why should it bother me if someone calls me something I'm not?"

The Fischers looked at Colin. Then they looked at Danny. Then, finally, at each other. After what seemed to Danny like a very long time (Colin timed it at seventeen seconds), Mrs. Fischer finally recovered the power of speech. "Danny," she breathed out, "go to your room and stay there. We'll talk about this in the morning."

"Aren't you going to make me say I'm sorry?"

Mr. Fischer put a hand on his wife's shoulder and regarded Danny. There was no anger on his face or in his voice. His shoulders slumped in a way that made him suddenly look smaller and older than his years. He was simply weary of it all. "You'll say it when you feel it. Now go."

Almost subliminal RELIEF flickered across Danny's face. Then he backed away and slowly closed the door to his own room. Colin observed he was careful to pull it shut quietly, guessing this was so as not to give the impression of resentment or defiance.

"Colin," Mr. Fischer said, gesturing toward the

---

27   Colin's excellent memory and early mastery of reading and mathematics made it difficult to test his IQ accurately, a frequent problem with child prodigies.

disaster area that just this morning had looked like Colin's bedroom. "Can we give you a hand with that? If we all work together, I'll bet we can put it to rights in no time."

Colin looked at his disordered room. When he spoke, the words came slowly and carefully. He was working hard not to lose control of himself again at the sight of it. "No, thank you. If it's all right, I'd like to do it myself. Good night."

"Okay," his mother reassured him. Her tone indicated more acceptance than approval of Colin's proclamation. "If you need anything, you know where to find us."

"Yes, I do. In the kitchen drinking wine or up in your room watching a premium cable show with violence and nudity."

With that, Colin stepped into his room and shut the door behind him.

Colin's anxiety and anger threatened to overwhelm him again as he surveyed the state of his belongings. While it appeared that nothing had actually been destroyed in Danny's ransacking, Colin had very particular ideas about where all of his things should go. At the end of a day that had pushed him far out of his comfort zone, the unexpected jolt of destruction to a place that had been safe and familiar to him was difficult to bear.

Colin forced himself to close his eyes, and then he

summoned a picture of how his room was supposed to look in its organized state. A quick mental inventory confirmed none of his belongings were actually missing. His stress levels reduced considerably.

Colin closed his eyes again. Now he was seeking to access his mental picture of the room and use it as a reference for returning things to their proper places. But to his surprise, he instead found his mind turning unbidden toward another memory entirely: the school cafeteria during the moment the gun went off.

Colin heard the deafening bang in the enclosed space. He felt his eardrums ring painfully. He smelled the acrid cordite from the cartridge as it overwhelmed the taste of carrots in his mouth. He saw students and even teachers running, in a panic. He saw the gun resting on the floor, pistol grip covered in pink and white-chocolate frosting.

For a moment, Colin wondered if he was suffering from post-traumatic stress disorder.[28] *No,* Colin concluded. While he was experiencing the memory of the gunshot and the chaos in the moments that followed, he wasn't attaching any negative emotions to it. He felt only the curiosity and desire to get to the bottom of the mystery.

Colin was certain that something was out of place

---

28 A psychological condition in which combat veterans and other witnesses to violent events find themselves constantly reliving the source of their trauma.

in the cafeteria that day, just as the contents of his room were out of place now. His memory rewound to the moments before the gun discharged, and Colin let his mind play over the details, no matter how small or unimportant they seemed. He remembered the sights, the smells, and the sounds. He pictured the people who were present, and what were they doing.

Unfortunately, as Colin knew, the human mind was an imperfect recording device. Instead of presenting things objectively, it emphasized the things it found most interesting. In Colin's case, this meant that his main memories of the moments before the gun went off involved Melissa Greer leaning over the table to invite him for cake . . . the scent of strawberries in her shampoo . . . her unexpectedly low, husky voice . . . the way her blouse hung as she leaned forward, affording him a view of her cleavage. . . .

Colin's eyes snapped open. He still didn't know what was out of place in the cafeteria that day. But it was enough to know something was amiss—it was enough to know something important was missing. He looked one more time at the pile of books and papers littering his carpet, then the remains of his social map. It seemed impossibly scattered. None of the relationships made sense anymore: Jocks were with nerds. Romances had become rivalries, rivalries friendships. Colin spotted the black triangle with *Wayne*'s name scrawled on it.

It had fallen into a corner by itself. As he returned it to the group, he saw that a photo of Rudy Moore had come to rest on top of the others. Something about the look on his face gave Colin that unsettling impression Rudy was staring at him. Colin moved away, but Rudy's eyes seemed to follow. Colin could not avoid the disturbing effect, no matter where he stood in his room. Finally, he turned the photo over. Leaving the rest of the map as it lay, Colin climbed into bed.

Moments later, the day's traumas not forgotten but compartmentalized, Colin fell into a deep sleep.

When Colin's parents awoke the next morning, they found their forgotten wineglasses had been covered in plastic and set on a high shelf. The kitchen was spotless. It smelled of bacon and French toast and hot syrup, and three places had been set with food to be eaten and juice to wash it down.

"Good morning," Colin said. He sat in a high-backed chair, reading the book on sharks his parents had given him as a child. "I made breakfast for everyone."

"Are you going to join us?" his father asked, impressed with the spread. He indicated the third place setting, inviting Colin to take a seat.

"Oh, no," Colin said. "I've already eaten."

He went back to reading, and his parents ate what he had prepared. Danny joined them a few minutes later, surprised to find something more complicated than Special K waiting for him. He never asked who was responsible for feeding him nor did he offer his thanks. He simply smiled with every bite, *HAPPY.* But it didn't matter, really.

Colin was already out the door and on his way to school.

CHAPTER TWELVE:
TEST BITES

When I was small, my father bought me a book on sharks and other dangerous sea creatures such as the killer whale and the giant squid. They were all very interesting. However, my favorite ocean-dwelling predator was always the great white shark.

At up to 20 feet in length and 5,000 lbs, mouth filled with serrated, dagger-like teeth, the great white (Carcharodon carcharias) is found in all the Earth's oceans. It is responsible for more attacks on humans than any other shark species. Given its size, ferocity, and status as an apex predator, this isn't surprising. What is surprising is that most of these attacks are nonfatal.

Scientists initially hypothesized that a human in the water, seen from below on a surf or paddleboard, would resemble the outline of a seal or sea lion—the great white shark's favorite meal. Since the shark's standard tactic is to ambush its prey with a quick, devastating bite and then wait as the unfortunate animal bleeds to death, the theory held that victims had time to haul themselves out of the water after the initial bite. Though widely accepted when first articulated, this theory has proved to be incorrect.

Further research revealed something unexpected: In most cases, great white sharks bite humans with only a tiny fraction of their usual two-thousand-pounds-per-foot of jaw strength. The truth is that most victims of great whites aren't being attacked at all. They're being subjected to "test bites." These light, probing bites are how a great white shark investigates strange or unfamiliar objects in its domain. An ungainly, bipedal land mammal attempting to swim in the ocean would indeed be strange and unfamiliar. Of course, a not insignificant number of those investigations do end in death from blood loss or decapitation, but this is to be expected.

When the investigator is a two-and-a-half-ton shark, even a gentle attempt at exploration can be fatal.

It was exactly noon when Colin again encountered Eddie and his friends.

Colin marched up the hall quickly and purposefully, Notebook clutched to his chest, glasses set squarely on the bridge of his nose. He knew that he had precisely two minutes and twenty-seven seconds before the second bell would ring and a bored teacher would shoo him into the cafeteria. The cafeteria was far too public a venue for what Colin now contemplated. In the wake of his encounter with *La Familia*, Colin had an entirely different set of questions for Eddie and his friends than what he had in mind just a day ago. They were questions he suspected Eddie might not like. Colin wanted to catch Eddie where he was weak and couldn't turn their conversation into a sideshow.

Colin heard Eddie before he saw him around the corner. He was with his friends, voice loud and boisterous, singsong in a way Colin associated with bragging—the kind that was generally a lie or at best an exaggeration.

". . . so anyway I'm like, 'What are you talking about? Your mom isn't even here,' " Eddie said to his friends, telling them a story. "So she did."

Eddie mimed zipping his pants down, grinning. His friends laughed. Colin had no idea what this meant and suspected some of Eddie's friends might not either. He edged closer, confident that he hadn't been seen.

"Whoa," Stan said. His voice had a slight nasal quality now, as the sound struggled to clear the swelling in his sinuses, indicated by the bandages over his nose.

"It was like I was the ice cream man or something," Eddie continued. *SMUG*.

"Or the ice cream." Stan grinned, showing the gap in his front teeth. Then he winced, presumably from pain induced by the sudden, broad movement in his facial muscles. Their friends laughed again.

"Hello, Eddie. How are you today?" Colin said. "I know the gun was yours."

The laughter stopped. Colin noted the sudden loss of color in Eddie's face, the way Stan looked the other direction, eyelids fluttering. These were clear signs of *GUILT*. The others just looked at each other and Colin with confused expressions—except for Cooper. He gave Colin his full attention, *INTERESTED* in hearing what Colin had to say.

Colin waited a moment for Eddie to reply, having been told again and again his own adherence to script sometimes prevented others from participating in conversation with him. Marie had explained how an uninterrupted barrage of information could make it so someone else "couldn't get a word in edgewise." His father referred to this as Colin "sucking up all the oxygen in the room." They both meant the same thing.

Even with this carefully measured conversational pause, Eddie issued no answer or denial. Colin processed the silence (factoring in the background cacophony of the hallway), assuring himself he'd given

Eddie sufficient edge and oxygen. "There is one thing I don't understand," Colin pushed on. "Why did you take the gun to the cafeteria?"

In preparing for this moment, Colin had anticipated many possible reactions, including violence (frightening—in which case Colin had been prepared to run) or an escape attempt (exciting—in which case Colin knew Eddie would eventually have to return home). The one reaction he didn't anticipate was the one his question elicited.

Eddie laughed.[29]

Colin had no idea what to make of this. The laughter was a mystery, especially since Eddie's facial expression no longer indicated NERVOUSNESS, but DELIGHT. Colin scribbled in his Notebook:

> Eddie laughs inappropriately when confronted. Question incorrectly phrased as a joke, or specific reference to gun carries some heretofore unknown sexual connotation? Investigate.

"Because I didn't, Brainiac," Eddie spat as Colin

---

29   Laughter is not a phenomenon limited to humans. Gorillas, chimpanzees, and other primates have been observed laughing for social purposes, as well as in response to tickling. Dogs and even rats also exhibit the behavior, although a rat laugh is so high-pitched that a human can't hear the sound. Colin found this very interesting, but he couldn't fathom what a rat or a dog might find funny. Most of the time, he had difficulty understanding jokes himself.

wrote. "I couldn't. I was in the weight room with the coach and half the football team. Getting burly."

Stan and his other friends nodded in agreement. After a moment, Cooper did too.

"You had to be in the cafeteria," Colin said. "That's where they found the gun. I saw it myself. There was birthday cake on the pistol grip." These were indisputable facts.

Stan's lips curled up in a smile that was in no way FRIENDLY. He stepped into Colin's space—a common power move designed to make a smaller boy shrink back or perhaps withdraw altogether. Colin, however, was too preoccupied with making sense of discontinuities between the facts to notice. Cooper smiled too. AMUSED.

"Trying to get your ass whooped again, Stan?" Cooper asked.

"Suck it," Stan hissed, focusing his attention on Colin but absently touching his broken nose, remembering what happened the last time he'd gotten this close. Without meaning to, he stopped in his tracks. "Look, Shortbus—"

"Don't call me that," Colin insisted. "I don't take the bus."

"—do yourself a favor and shut up while you're ahead. Or the janitor will find you hanging on a coat hook by your Fruit of the Looms." Stan let the threat hang in the air, looming over Colin, his teeth bared like a dog. Or perhaps a chimpanzee.[30]

Colin considered Stan, fixated on his front teeth, then flipped back a few pages in his Notebook. He looked between Stan's angry visage and whatever he had written there. "No," he announced finally. "Aside from the person who bought the gun, *El Cocodrilo* referenced a 'gap-toothed freak.' I'm 99 percent certain he meant you."

Cooper and the others snickered at Stan's expense, a turn Colin recognized as dangerous. Whatever unconscious respect Stan might have had for Colin's unpredictable but demonstrably dangerous right hook evaporated in the face of humiliation at the hands of his peers. He took another step forward, balling his fists, leaning in for the fight.

A delicate female hand suddenly grabbed Colin by the shoulder and yanked him backward. Colin yelped with surprise. He suppressed his instinctive urge to fight or flee as he processed the familiar and welcome scent of strawberry shampoo.

---

30 In spite of their depiction as gentle companions to human beings in film and television, chimpanzees are widely considered among the most vicious and dangerous of primates. People who have adopted them routinely report chimpanzee attacks on other household pets or even members of the family. Invariably, these animals are consigned to zoos or put down. Even so, Colin secretly hoped a chimpanzee would appear at the window and give him the finger every time a truck passed the Fischers on the freeway.

"Colin," Melissa said with a sigh. She pulled him behind her, subtly interposing herself between Colin and imminent danger. "Stop."

Stan jabbed a ragged, nail-bitten finger at Melissa. "Outta the way," he growled. "Just because you're hot now doesn't mean you're in charge."

Melissa and Colin both puzzled over this one. Colin knew that while high-value female members of social species often wielded some respect and authority, it was most often because she was associated with a higher-ranking male or performed the duties of protecting and instructing younger pack members. Melissa clearly didn't meet the latter condition, other than the occasional babysitting job.

"I know Colin talks a lot," Melissa admitted. "He says things he probably shouldn't say. But he can't help it. He . . . he has a *condition*."

Eddie shook his head as Stan looked to him for advice and possibly instruction. "Whatever," he finally proclaimed. "Just make sure Rain Man here controls his mouth."

"Rain Man was autistic." Colin frowned. "I'm—"

"Coming to the cafeteria with me," Melissa said. She herded Colin away from the scene as the bell started to ring. For the first time in his life, Colin did not respond to the sound in any way. In fact, he did not notice it at all.

"But—" Colin tried to protest, looking back at Eddie. Feeling FRUSTRATED.

"I want some ice cream."

Behind them, Eddie and his friends just laughed. Colin still didn't know why.

Ever since he could remember, Colin had been making weekly visits to the Griffith Park Observatory with his parents. As scientists and engineers in the space program, the Fischers felt a special connection to the place. Colin's mother once told him that these visits reminded her why her job was worth it, even on the days when she wished everyone she worked with would drop dead.

This meant nothing to Colin. He simply enjoyed the view and the breeze that seemed to blow constantly. And having no fear of heights, he loved to run to the rails and peer over the side at the city below. Often, Mrs. Fischer would lift him up to the pay binoculars so he could enjoy a better look. "Take it all in, Big C," she would say to him. "There's life on this planet we call Earth."

One particular afternoon when Colin was three, he stood near the observatory with a bottle of soap in his hand, blowing bubbles high into the air. Colin liked to watch the bubbles rise on the wind, refracting the setting sunlight into dozens of tiny rainbow spheres.

Each seemed a world unto itself—perhaps a universe—until they dissipated. He wondered who lived there and if they were sad when their bubble popped.

It was as he had paused to blow a fresh bouquet of rainbows into the sky that Colin felt tiny arms reach around his waist. Surprised, he turned and saw a little girl smiling at him. He took note of her bright blue eyes, perfect round teeth, and the smell of strawberries in her hair. He was so struck by her, he dropped his soap bubble bottle. As the clear liquid spilled onto the concrete, the little girl did something that Colin—who could conceive of whole civilizations encompassed by soap bubbles—could not properly imagine. . . . She kissed him. Then she ran away.

Colin screamed then like a wounded animal, unsettled by the unwelcome touch and most especially the uninvited kiss. When his mother arrived, breathless and panicked at her son's cry of distress, she saw the soap spill and the half-empty bottle rolling toward the curb. She did not see the little girl dashing for her mother or the look the girl cast back at her son. "It's okay," Mrs. Fischer reassured him. "We'll buy you more bubbles."

Colin never forgot those eyes or the smell of her hair.

Then, as now, Colin couldn't take his eyes off of Melissa. She picked at her Salisbury steak, occasionally lifting the barest forkful to her lips. He watched her chew, lost in thought as he worked through the meaning of his confrontation with Eddie. She caught his eye, then looked away. Inexplicably, she appeared EMBARRASSED.

"Sorry about what I said to Eddie and those guys about you," Melissa offered between bird-like bites. "I just—I wanted them to leave you alone."

"You're barely touching your food."

"You're mad at me. I can tell."

Colin wrinkled his nose, wondering how Melissa could tell he was MAD when he was in fact not MAD at all. Nor was Colin aware of anything he should be MAD about. "I wouldn't be mad at you for not eating your lunch," he replied.

"Not my *lunch*," Melissa explained. "What I *said*."

"Oh." Colin nodded as though this made perfect sense. "What did you say?"

"I said I was sorry."

"Oh." He carefully separated his carrots from his celery. "For what?"

Melissa smiled. It was that same mysterious smile from so long ago. The same smile she had occasionally offered since she had kissed him that day at the observatory. He could not name it. The smile eluded him.

"You're smiling," Colin observed. "That means you feel better, and maybe now you can eat your Salisbury steak." He popped a carrot in his mouth as he spoke.

"Colin," Melissa said with a frown, pointing to her lips. Was she inviting him to kiss her? This seemed unlikely and unsanitary. It could only mean he was chewing with his mouth open, as usual, and Melissa was helpfully pointing this out. People did not enjoy watching others chew their food. It was a habit that Colin had to be conscious of while eating, but this was difficult when his mind was on other, More Important Things.

"Thank you," he said after swallowing and before taking another bite.

Melissa shrugged. "Anyway, it's not that. I just don't like to have a lot at once. I like to eat a little at a time."

Colin nodded—this was wise. He knew several small meals a day were actually better for you. They gave the body a constant influx of calories and kept the metabolism stable. He would have said all of this, but his mouth was full of carrots again. "That's how a shark eats," he said as he considered a celery stick. "Don't let the movies fool you; a harbor seal is not a very big meal."

"Yeah. I try to stay away from harbor seal sandwiches, myself."

"No, really," Colin insisted. "A shark will store food in his stomach for months, perfectly preserved. That's why when you see one that's been killed on the news, they talk about things they find inside. Entire limbs, sometimes even pieces of a head shredded by the shark's teeth and crushed by its esophagus. The shark is just saving it for later." He bit the celery with a crunch and tore away a chunk. It amused him to imagine he was a shark, and the celery was his prey.

Suddenly, Melissa found the Salisbury steak even less appetizing than she had just moments before. She set down her fork and pushed her tray away from her.

Colin chewed, forgetting once again to keep his mouth closed. "That doesn't even count the random things a shark will swallow and keep down there. They found an entire outboard motor in one great white. It just spilled out when they split open his stomach, and the funny thing is it still worked." He tore off another bite of his celery, jaws working as fast as his mind now. "In another one, they found a . . ."

Colin stopped speaking. Colin stopped chewing. It was all very un-Colin-like.

Melissa rose, concerned, her horror at his lunchtime dissertation forgotten as she leaned across the lunch table. "Colin? *Colin*," she said, scooting closer and weighing the risks of touching him, "are you okay?"

"Birthday cake," Colin said. "And a gun."

CHAPTER THIRTEEN:
WHAT THE TORTOISE SAID TO ACHILLES

"The Tortoise and the Hare" is among the most well-known of Aesop's fables. It goes like this: One day, a tortoise challenged a hare to a race. The hare, knowing he was much faster than the slow, lumbering tortoise, readily agreed. When the race began, the hare sprinted to an early and apparently insurmountable lead. He became so confident in victory he decided to rest. But the hare fell fast asleep, and the tortoise overtook him.

When the hare awoke, he realized the tortoise had almost reached the finish line. The hare dashed ahead, faster than he had ever run, scarcely able to believe his friend the tortoise could possibly defeat him. But the hare had woken up too late. He could not run fast enough. The tortoise had won. The moral of the story is generally interpreted as "slow and steady wins the race."

Author Lewis Carroll turned this moral on its ear. In an 1885 dialogue, the tortoise explains to Achilles that no matter how fast Achilles runs, he can never defeat the tortoise in a race. Through a series of logical propositions, he proves to Achilles that once a lead is taken, it cannot be overcome. In short, if Achilles can only close half the lead between the tortoise and himself at a time, he is doomed to remain behind.

Carroll was not attempting to reach a moral conclusion but illustrate a paradox: Sometimes, logical deductions do not match real world experience. Sometimes, even the most logical person presented with the most objective evidence must put mathematics aside and embrace what he observes to be true. This is called an "inference," and it is the only way to resolve Carroll's paradox. An inference exists beyond logic and reason.

Inferences make me uncomfortable because I like certainty. The risk of faulty logic is the emergence of a paradox that might someday be resolved through better logic; the risk of making a faulty inference is that you're simply wrong. However, an inference can be useful. Of all the most basic questions posed to any investigator,

> inference can answer the most difficult. Not who,
> what, when, where, or how ... but why.
>   "Why" can be the most important question of
> all because human behavior isn't always logical.
> Human behavior is not a mystery that can be
> solved or fully understood in mathematical terms.
> It just has to be experienced.

Dr. Doran walked briskly up the front hallway toward the main office, heels clicking against the tile, her eyes narrowed and jaw set. She was marching into a battle she did not choose, but intended to win. And God help anyone who kept her from it.

Wayne Connelly's voice echoed out into the hallway. "I told you," he was saying to the secretary, "I'm here to see Dr. Doran."

Dr. Doran moved in behind him with her arms crossed, a formidable presence. Wayne knew from the look on the secretary's face and the prickling of the hair on the back of his neck that he should turn around.[31] The boy who imagined himself afraid of nothing was, in his heart, as afraid as he had ever been.

31　Many experiments have actually been carried out to determine the existence of the so-called psychic staring effect, most notably by biochemist and fringe researcher Rupert Sheldrake. Sheldrake found that blindfolded test subjects could detect when someone was staring at them at rates consistently above what could be accounted for by random chance. A handful of subjects answered correctly every time. Michael Shermer and others from the skeptic community attempted to debunk Sheldrake's results by pointing to potential bias on the part of the

"You were told to stay off-campus, period." Somehow, her lack of emotion was scarier to Wayne than his stepfather Ken's white-hot rage. "I didn't want to handle things this way, but you don't leave me much choice. The police are on the way, and they'll take it—and you—from here."

Wayne felt heavy, his limbs leaden. His head slumped down toward his chest, and he could not stop it no matter how hard he tried. It was all so desperately unfair; he knew that no matter what he said, he would not be believed. No one cared.

"Good," Colin said, appearing from practically nowhere at the office door.

Wayne found the strength to lift his eyes toward Colin, betrayal and confusion stinging them. Dr. Doran took a step to the side so she could stare down both boys at once. She was no more certain of Colin's intentions or his meaning than Wayne was.

Colin stood tall, arms straight. His glasses seemed to sit right on his nose. He did not slouch, or slump, or look away. For the first time in his life, he didn't look like a boy who could be bullied or in need of protection from bullies. Colin looked CERTAIN.

"The police will be here when Wayne is proved innocent," Colin said.

Sandy entered behind Colin, as confused by the

---

experimenters. However, Sheldrake's findings were reproduced by other researchers who altered their methods to answer skeptics' objections.

gathering as anyone. "Dr. Doran?" she asked. "I got a note that you wanted to see me?"

Dr. Doran looked between Colin and Wayne and then at Sandy, suddenly understanding why Sandy had come even if she didn't understand the reason behind the invitation. "I didn't send anybody a note. If you got one, it was forged." She directed the word *forged* at Colin, as if to say, "We're going to talk."

Colin shook his head, clearly disagreeing with Dr. Doran's conclusion. "The note only said that you want to see her, which you do, even if you don't know it yet. I know this because I sent the note."

Dr. Doran took a deep, cleansing breath. "Colin, I told you before: There are limits to my indulgence of you."

"I told you before: The gun didn't belong to Wayne. And I was right."

Sandy shifted nervously. She edged back toward the door. "Can I go?"

"Go, Sandy," Dr. Doran said.

"*Stay*, Sandy," Colin said.

"Wake up, Wayne," Wayne said. He slapped his own cheek, hard.

Colin was acutely aware of the SHOCK that rippled through the office from his clear but simple defiance. He could feel the stares directed at him, the CONFUSION and ANGER of the teachers and staff, the ADMIRATION of his fellow students. None of that mattered. None of that could be allowed to distract him from his mission now.

Sandy had gone pale. She shook with FEAR.

Colin turned to her. There was no malice in him. No cruelty. There was just a relentless confidence in the facts. "It was Eddie's gun," Colin explained. "He bought it from a *La Familia* in Sylmar named *El Cocodrilo*, which is Spanish for 'The Crocodile.' They call him this on account of his toothy smile. I think that's a bad metaphor because crocodiles can't smile.[32] But it's his name, and I suppose he can call himself whatever he likes."

"Dude," Wayne interjected, "if you could get to the point, that would kick ass."

"Yes," Dr. Doran agreed, ignoring his language. "Less color, more fact."

"Eddie bought the gun because he was mad at Wayne and wanted to scare him. But he never got the chance," Colin revealed. He fixed his gaze on Sandy, not letting the FEAR in her eyes stop him. "You took it out of his locker when he wasn't looking and you hid it in your purse."

"That—that's crazy," Sandy stammered.

"No, it's perfectly rational. You took the gun to protect Eddie because you like him. The same reason why you ate ice cream with him when your mother wasn't home."

---

32 Crocodiles have a habit of lying on a riverbank with their mouths wide open, displaying twenty-four jagged teeth. This was thought to be a "smile" by some observers and a show of aggression by others. Zoologists, however, discovered that crocodiles sweat through their mouths. Smiling is just how a crocodile stays cool.

Whatever color remained in Sandy's face drained away. She seemed to know what Colin was referring to, but no one else did. Colin himself only understood it in the context of Eddie's story. Not even Wayne, schooled as he was in the dark arts of schoolyard innuendo, could say for certain what ice cream had to do with anything.

"You can't prove anything," Sandy croaked past the lump in her throat.

Dr. Doran stepped between Colin and Sandy. She had seen and heard quite enough, and if there was more to hear, the main office wasn't the place for it. "Sandy is right," she said to Colin. "And without proof, you're just harassing an innocent student."

"Like Wayne?" Colin asked.

"Don't change the subject."

"I'm not. Wayne *is* the subject. And the gun." He gestured toward Sandy and the large purse slung over her shoulder. "Look inside her purse. You'll find residual gun oil and some pink-and-white-chocolate frosting, from the piece with the rose."

In spite of herself, Dr. Doran glanced down at Sandy's open purse. Was that dried chocolate frosting crusted on the inside? It was hard to say.

"You saved a piece of Melissa Greer's birthday cake to take to Eddie after his workout," Colin reminded Sandy. "The gun must have rubbed against it as it fell out during the disturbance in the cafeteria. Just like your tube of melon lipstick, which you had to replace."

Wayne just stared at Colin. This was the most amazing thing he had seen in a week of amazing things. He made a surreptitious attempt to gain Colin's attention and share the moment, but Colin was oblivious to Wayne's sudden swell of camaraderie.

Sandy shook her head in denial and disbelief. She glared at Colin, her *FEAR* transforming into *HATE*. As an adolescent girl, hate was a weapon she knew how to use. "I don't have to say anything to you . . . *Shortbus*."

"Don't call him that," Wayne growled before he realized he had said anything at all. Dr. Doran frowned. If Colin noticed the slur, it made no difference.

"I already spoke to Eddie," Colin pressed. "He knows what you did." The first assertion was a fact, the second a strongly stated conjecture. Still, there was no way to know whether Colin was telling the truth to manipulate Sandy's response or not. His expression was blank, his voice emotionless. He was a walking, talking Kuleshov Effect.

"Tell the truth or take the consequences. I know it seems like you'll be better off if you don't say anything, but it's not true. The math just isn't on your side." He stepped closer to her, unconscious of encroaching on Sandy's personal space in a way that under other circumstances would have been impossible for him. "Tell the truth now before the police get here," he insisted. "And maybe you won't go to jail."

"That's it," Dr. Doran broke in, and she meant it. "We're done here."

"But we have to bring Eddie in. We have to ask him how he made contact with *La Familia* and arranged for the purchase. This is much bigger than—"

"*Enough.*"

Colin was silenced by her intensity—even taken aback. "Dr. Doran . . ."

"He was so mad at Wayne," Sandy broke in suddenly, staring out the window. She sounded strange, disconnected from everything and everyone. Even the fear seemed to have fled from her as the words flooded out. "I didn't know what he would do. I couldn't let him hurt anyone, and I couldn't let him get in trouble." She looked over to Dr. Doran, pleading now. "Please don't let me go to jail."

Dr. Doran's eyes flicked toward the picture window on the far side of the office, behind the secretaries' desks. Outside, she could see what Sandy had been staring at the entire time she'd been speaking: A police cruiser was parked in the driveway now. A pair of LAPD school policemen were making their way to the front door.

"Sandy, get in my office and call your parents," Dr. Doran snapped. "Call them right now." Sandy didn't have to be spoken to again; she did as she was instructed and disappeared down the narrow hallway to Dr. Doran's private office. Dr. Doran waited for her to close the door behind her, then fixed on Wayne and Colin. Hers was not the look of an authority figure grateful for the efforts of private citizens.

"Wayne, go home. We'll work this out tomorrow. And Colin . . ." Her voice trailed off. She was less certain about how to deal with Colin than she was about anything in this sea of uncertainties she found herself swimming in.

"No need to thank me," Colin said helpfully. "We will deal with Eddie next."

"You missed detention yesterday. Now you owe me two."

With that, she turned on her heel and marched out of the office to intercept the police before the situation got any bigger or any worse. Wayne watched her go, waiting for the click of her heels to fade to inaudibility before daring to address Colin.

"Dude," Wayne said finally. "That blows."

Colin slumped ever so slightly. His glasses slipped, and he pushed them back up. This was not how he expected all of this to end. Later, in his Notebook he observed:

> Real life doesn't work like a mystery novel. But it should. ~~Investigate.~~

"It's quiet in detention," Colin said. "I like it when it's quiet."

CHAPTER FOURTEEN:
HANS ASPERGER

The subcategory of autistic spectrum disorders called Asperger's syndrome takes its name from Hans Asperger, an Austrian pediatrician who did most of his work in Vienna during the 1930s and '40s. As a child, Asperger himself displayed many traits of the syndrome that bears his name. Shy, remote, and lonely, Asperger had a gift for languages and an astonishing memory for subjects he was interested in and would often bore and alienate his classmates with recitations of long passages by his favorite poet.

As an adult working with disabled children, he was fascinated by a group of patients he called his "little professors"—socially awkward boys and girls who would fixate on a subject and talk about it passionately and in great detail. While mainstream *autism researchers in the United States focused on these patients' disabilities, Asperger emphasized their special talents and their potential for great contributions to society in adulthood. "They fulfill their role well," he wrote, "perhaps better than anyone else could, and we are talking of people who as children had the greatest difficulties and caused untold worries to their caregivers."*

Only later did researchers realize Asperger had another motive for emphasizing his patients' gifts rather than their deficiencies: his desire to save their lives. While he was careful never to lie, he managed to artfully arrange the facts in a way to best make his case to the Nazi authorities in Vienna that his patients did indeed have lives worthy of living. As a scientist, Asperger felt a commitment to the truth. As a doctor, he felt an even greater commitment to the welfare of the children in his care.

This is why I would not make a very good doctor. I have a difficult time making decisions under pressure. Especially when there are consequences.

Dinner at the Fischer house that night was uncharacteristically quiet.

"So, Big C. I got a call from your principal today," Mrs. Fischer finally said, breaking the silence.

Colin had a good idea what Dr. Doran had said but

decided the best policy was to wait until his mother had revealed her hand. Though he was not an experienced liar, Colin had long ago mastered the art of compartmentalizing information. It was a time-honored investigative technique with proven results.

"Detention," she finished. "Two days in a row."

"Yes," Colin acknowledged, as though she had just made a comment about the dress code or school supplies. He picked up an asparagus stalk, experimentally bending it between his fingers, testing the point at which it snapped in two. "I like asparagus," he said. "Although there is one thing I do not like, and that is it makes my pee smell funny."

"You plan to tell us what happened?" Mr. Fischer asked. "Or are you just gonna sit there and finish your asparagus?"

Colin did not answer. If anything, he focused even more intently on testing the tensile strength of his vegetables. "Chemists think it has to do with the digestive system breaking down sulfur compounds into ammonia, but they're not really sure."

"Dr. Doran told us everything," his father revealed, undeterred by Colin's efforts to change the subject. "She said—Colin, look at me—she said you got into a fight. Then you skipped detention. Then you lied to her, forged a note from the office, and fooled Wayne into coming into school when he was clearly forbidden from doing so. LAPD had to dispatch a cruiser to West Valley High, for God's sake."

Mrs. Fischer looked at her husband very seriously. "Salt, please?" she asked. He passed it to her without comment. "Thanks," she said, and dashed it over her potatoes.

Colin cut into his asparagus, took a bite, and chewed very slowly, working to keep his face as blank as possible.

His father, pointing his fork across the table for emphasis, made no such effort. Still, it was difficult to say if he was ANGRY or IMPRESSED—his expression kept changing, as though he didn't know how he felt himself. "In forty-eight hours, you've broken more rules, started more trouble, and caused more chaos than in all your fourteen years on this planet."

Danny squirmed in his chair, drumming the table with his hands. "Yes!" he hissed under his breath, but not quite under his breath enough. One dark look from his mother was all it took to silence him immediately. Danny returned to eating his salmon.

"You also saved an innocent boy."

Colin chewed his asparagus five more times, swallowed, and then washed down what remained of the mouthful with a sip of chilled water. "No, I didn't," Colin said. "I just figured out the truth. The rest . . . happened."

"Either way, we're proud of you."

"And if you ever do it again," his mother said, raising a warning finger, "we'll strap you to a chair, lock you in a closet, and feed you through a tube."

Colin understood she was exaggerating for effect, and the punishment described was an unlikely outcome whether or not he did anything like this again. However, he knew with equal certainty whatever consequence his mother actually devised would be, in its own way, far less entertaining. Colin nodded, acknowledging her threat as he went back to his dinner, quietly hoping this discussion was at an end. After all, he suspected this was all far from over. There were still too many questions.

"Colin," Mr. Fischer said.

"Yes, Dad?"

"You were saying. About asparagus."

"Oh," Colin said. He looked at his father and pushed his glasses up his nose. "What is very interesting is that while everyone seems to produce the compounds for stinky asparagus urine, only about half the population can detect the smell. . . ."

An hour later, Colin sat in his room, enjoying the solitude as he recorded his thoughts for the day in his Notebook. His quiet repose was interrupted by the approach of familiar footsteps and the creak of his door.

Danny stood at the entrance for a moment, giving

Colin an *UNCERTAIN* look. "So that's pretty cool what you did," he said.

Colin had no idea what Danny was talking about.

"Nailing Sandy Ryan for bringing that gun," Danny explained, *EXASPERATED*. "I guess she deserved it for peeing on your bed."

"No," Colin said, "she deserved it for not reporting the gun to the authorities."

Danny shook his head, quite certain he would never really understand his older brother. "Speaking of which . . . about messing up your room. You remember how Dad said I would apologize to you when I really felt it?"

"Yes."

"Just wanted to see if you remembered that," Danny said. "Later, loser."

Danny left. Colin wasn't sure why, but he was overcome with the urge to smile.

Dr. Doran had arranged for Sandy and her mother to come before the first bell so she could clear out her locker before most of the other students arrived. Melissa, who had arrived early, watched from a distance as her friend peeled stickers off the metal and collected her things into a cardboard box. Sandy paused only to wipe away her tears.

Melissa sensed Colin standing behind her. He was

watching the scene with mild curiosity, his Notebook open, recording his thoughts on the matter.

> 7:30 A.M.: Sandy Ryan cries as she clears out her locker, including the following items:
> —A poster of a teenage singer whose high-pitched voice makes me cringe.
> —Photographs of herself with various friends, including Melissa and Eddie. In the picture of Eddie, she is kissing him on the cheek. Eddie looks bored. I am not sure if he is bored with Sandy, the kiss, or where she is kissing him.
> —Stickers. Most depict rainbows, unicorns, or shirtless men with rippling muscles.
> —A dog-eared copy of a novel about a girl who becomes romantically involved with a zombie. (I do not understand this at all. Zombies eat people; they do not kiss girls.)
> —Eddie's blue-and-gold Notre Dame jacket.
> Since Sandy has never been what I would describe as an academic, I assume she is not sad for the loss of West Valley High School's myriad scholastic opportunities. Her tears seem to coincide with the removal of specific artifacts. Nostalgia? Will she miss her friends? I find this unlikely. Sandy is not moving out of the neighborhood, and her popularity with

> upperclassmen affords easy access to private
>
> transportation—

"I can't believe it," Melissa said softly, interrupting Colin's thought. "Expelled."

"She had a gun," Colin said. "It was in her purse."

"Eddie's gun." Melissa gestured with her chin, drawing his attention to Eddie. He stood at the other end of the hall with a knot of his friends. They were usually the loudest and most boisterous students in the school, but this morning they were quiet—especially Eddie. Colin wrote all of this down.

> Eddie watches Sandy clear out her locker. He
>
> does not help. He looks SAD. Sandy must know he is
>
> there, but she does not look at him.

"He doesn't get so much as a detention," Melissa said. "It's not fair."

"Oh," Colin said. "Is that why she is crying?"

"Of course it is. It's not fair, and she knows it. Anyone would cry."

"It's not about what's fair," Colin said as he wrote this down. "It's about what can be proved by the evidence. The police can't prove the gun belonged to Eddie."

Melissa turned to face him. She was close enough for Colin to be acutely aware that while her left eye was blue like Colin's, her right had a nearly imperceptible greenish tint—a condition called heterochromia. Colin wondered if she started life in the womb as a twin and then absorbed her brother or sister into her own body early in her mother's pregnancy, a phenomenon that was sometimes responsible for chimerism.[33]

Then Colin felt a strange sensation. He realized Melissa was holding his hand. In fact, she most likely had been holding it for the last few seconds, as he had pondered the circumstances of her conception. He did not recall her touching him.

"You could," she said.

With that, the first bell rang. Melissa squeezed Colin's hand once, then headed off to her first class of the day. Colin looked down at his hand—he could still see faint impressions of Melissa's fingers on his skin. He walked down the corridor, staring at his hand, watching the mark she had left upon him slowly fade.

All thoughts of Melissa suddenly fled as Colin felt his body slam into a locker.

The locker's dial dug into his back, and his ears

---

33 Chimerism is a condition wherein a single organism derives traits from multiple, fused zygotes. For example, an Olympic cyclist accused of blood doping contended that blood cells found in his body with DNA different than his own were actually produced by an absorbed fraternal twin. And a woman who needed a kidney transplant discovered that her adult children who had themselves tested for genetic compatibility were not actually hers. They were the product of ovarian tissue from a "sister" who had vanished in the womb.

rang from the impact. Colin winced, closing his eyes to block out the pain. He started to count. When he opened his eyes again, he saw Stan's face, six inches from his own. Stan was ANGRY.

Stan breathed so hard, the bandages that covered his nose bloomed red from the blood vessel he had just reopened. Colin was fascinated by the sticky, scarlet fractal pattern spreading through the ragged weave of gauze.[34] "You shouldn't get so angry," Colin said. "You could hurt yourself again."

Stan grabbed Colin by his jacket with both hands and slammed him against the locker again. Colin's teeth rattled. "You think you're funny, Shortbus?"

"I'm going to be late to class," Colin said, and tried to step away.

Eddie blocked his path. If anything, he looked even ANGRIER than Stan. Cooper and three of Stan's other friends hovered behind him. Colin calculated the boys had positioned themselves to cut off any other avenue of escape.

"Good," Eddie rasped. "So is Sandy. Like, for the

---

34 Fractal geometry is a branch of mathematics that is used primarily to understand recursive processes. A "fractal" is an irregular polygon that appears roughly the same at any scale, from the infinitesimal to the infinite. This property is referred to as "self-similarity," which refers to the repetition of statistical features. These concepts as they apply to chaos theory were popularized in the novel and movie about dinosaurs run amok, *Jurassic Park*. Colin appreciated the special effects but quibbled with the title since half the dinosaurs on display were actually from the Cretaceous period.

rest of her life." He grabbed Colin, twisting the top of his shirt in his fists, winching him up off his feet.

"Don't touch me," Colin said, his breath coming faster now. "I—"

"I know. You don't like to be touched. Well, *boo-hoo*, you little bitch—what are you gonna do, kick my ass? One sucker punch doesn't make you Jet Li."

Stan touched his own nose, not noticing the smear of blood that rubbed off onto his finger. "Yeah," Stan repeated. "You're not Jet Li."

"He doesn't need Jet Li."

Wayne stepped around the corner, a half smile hanging on his face. The smile suggested to Colin that whatever Wayne was planning to do next, Wayne believed he was going to enjoy it. A lot.

Eddie laughed. "Get over yourself. You're never gonna take all of us."

"No, Eddie," Wayne said. "Just you."

CRUEL, Colin decided. Wayne's smile was definitely CRUEL. For some reason, this didn't bother Colin in the slightest.

Eddie released Colin, letting him drop to the tile. He and Stan made fists. Wayne simply stood, his body relaxed but completely alert.

"Wayne is very strong," Colin said as he slipped past Stan and Eddie to Wayne's side. "His muscles have clearly developed at an accelerated rate. A combination of diet, genetics, and environmental conditions probably forced him into early puberty. If you look at his upper lip, you'll see that he—"

Wayne cleared his throat. "Colin. Bio lecture later, okay?"

"Okay." In his Notebook, Colin opened to a fresh page and recorded a reminder to *explain the development of secondary sexual characteristics in early adolescence to Wayne at a mutually convenient time.*

No one on either side of the face-off spoke or even moved for the next twenty-five seconds. Colin knew this because he maintained a silent count and recorded it in his Notebook. The confrontation ended only when the tardy bell rang, which Colin found slightly disappointing—he was curious to see how long this could continue.

A history teacher with gray, frizzy hair stuck her head out of her classroom. "Get to class, you animals," she barked, then slammed her door shut.

Eddie looked one last time at Colin and Wayne before he turned to Stan, Cooper, and the others. With a nod of his head, the other boys dispersed in silence. Colin and Wayne were left standing alone in the hallway. "Hey," Wayne said.

"Good morning, Wayne. How are you today?"

Wayne paused for seven seconds. "You doing anything after school?"

"I have detention."

"I mean, after that."

Colin furrowed his brow, deep in thought as he

reviewed his schedule. Then his face suddenly brightened. He had an idea, and it seemed like a very good one. "Do you like trampolines?" he asked.

Wayne shrugged. There was really only one way to find out.

CHAPTER FIFTEEN:
TWO DOCTORS IN VIENNA

While Hans Asperger did his pioneering work in Vienna's University Children's Hospital, another pediatric psychiatrist named Heinrich Gross was doing work of his own barely a mile away in the Am Spiegelgrund Children's Clinic. Children at the clinic remembered Dr. Gross walking the hallways in his crisp brown uniform with the swastika armband. He took particular interest in those diagnosed with the physical, mental, and behavioral disabilities that led the Nazi authorities to designate them as "unclean."

Gross and his colleagues were performing experiments on these children and then murdering them, usually through drug overdoses, starvation, or exposing them to the elements until they caught fatal pneumonia. More than eight hundred children died at Spiegelgrund in this fashion—"lives unworthy of life," as the Nazis called them.

Meanwhile, Dr. Asperger argued passionately for the social usefulness of his patients. He emphasized the extraordinary abilities that often accompanied their handicaps. Families of children whom Asperger treated were struck by his sensitivity and compassion. Many of his patients went on to live happy, successful lives, including Elfriede Jelinek, who would one day win the Nobel Prize in Literature.

In late 1944, Asperger's clinic was destroyed in a bombing raid by the Allies. His colleague Sister Victorine was killed. Most of his research was lost. Asperger's work had been largely forgotten when he died in relative obscurity in 1981.

Fellow physician Gross escaped prosecution at the end of the Second World War. He went on to become one of Austria's most distinguished physicians, even winning the nation's highest honor for medicine. For several decades, Gross continued neurological research on the preserved brains of the children he had helped murder. Only toward the end of his life in the early 2000s was Gross prosecuted for war crimes—a trial that was dismissed because of the accused's alleged senility. He finally died in 2005.

The remains of Gross's victims were formally

cremated in a memorial ceremony in 2002, and he died free but recognized for the monster he was. Asperger's reputation was rehabilitated when his work was rediscovered and translated into English in the 1990s. The syndrome that bears his name has become a household word.

My father says that Heinrich Gross was simply evil, and some people are like that. I'm not sure if I can accept this explanation. Try as I might, I can't understand how so much horror can be encompassed by such a tiny word. I told my father this once, and he asked me to consider how so much good is encompassed by a word as tiny as "love."

Colin had only served detention once before, over a misunderstanding involving the Case of the Talking Doll. He had been conducting a noisy experiment with the motion sensor that caused the subject doll to bark like a dog instead of say "Mama" or "I love you." His homeroom teacher, Ms. Breyman, thought Colin was intentionally disrupting class and gave him a stern warning. When Colin pointed out that homeroom was not in fact a class, and therefore there was nothing to disrupt, Ms. Breyman gave him lunch detention. Colin didn't think this was fair, but Marie pointed out that sometimes fairness was a difficult balancing act when attempting to maintain basic social order.

"She's your teacher," Marie had said. "She has thirty students to worry about. If they all talked back to her, where would she be?"

"Her classroom," Colin replied. He didn't understand why Marie laughed.

Today, detention was not to be served in peace and quiet in the classroom of an aging teacher who simply wanted to grade papers. Mr. Turrentine was on detention duty. Unlike many of his peers, Mr. Turrentine believed detention—as with any punishment—was an instructional opportunity. He took instruction very seriously.

Colin stood alone in Mr. Turrentine's office. The gym itself was smelly and dirty, but Colin was beginning to admire his teacher's sense of order. It wasn't just the way the gym equipment all seemed to find its way back exactly where it belonged at the end of each class (every ball, for example, was numbered such that it was assigned to a specific rack and had to be arranged in a specific, ordinal sequence), but everything in the gym seemed to have a place. This was even truer in Turrentine's inner sanctum.

Mr. Turrentine had lists for everything. Equipment, supplies, and students—it didn't matter; it was all tracked, labeled, and categorized. There was a clipboard for every class, with every student's name, the day in the semester, and a "✓" or an "✗" on a grid. Fascinated, Colin found his period and scanned the list of names until he found his own:

Fischer, C.M. followed by seven ✓ marks. Colin smiled. He looked for his friends and people he knew, eager to compare their performance. **Greer, M.A.** also had seven check marks. **Connelly, W.J.** had seven ✗'s. It was as Colin's finger alighted on the listing for **Moore, R.T.** that he heard Mr. Turrentine clear his throat behind him.

"Are you my personal assistant, Fischer?" Mr. Turrentine asked.

"No," Colin replied, turning.

"Are you a helpful gnome who cleans my desk, organizes my files, and shines my shoes at night so that I don't have to?"

"No," Colin said. "I am not."

"That is correct, Fischer. You are none of those things. So would you care to explain to me why, in the name of all that is good and holy, you would be in my office poking your nose in my belongings?" Mr. Turrentine stared down at him, his hands resting on his hips. Strangely, he did not look ANGRY.

"I'm here because this is the first of two detentions I've been assigned. The first was for fighting in class—you were there—the second was for proving that Sandy Ryan brought the gun into the cafeteria and not Wayne Connelly. But I'm not supposed to talk about any of that for legal reasons. You understand."

"I do."

"Mr. Turrentine," Colin asked, "where do I sit?"

"Sit?" Mr. Turrentine turned on his heel. He did not beckon to Colin or do anything other than expect to be followed, and Colin complied. They marched out into the auxiliary gym, where Colin found a line of students in their regular clothes lined up and standing at attention. "Get in line, Fischer," Mr. Turrentine barked. So Colin did.

Colin was keenly aware that he knew no one in this line. Most were upperclassmen, and physically Colin was the smallest. The boy next to him smelled like feet. Colin scrunched up his nose to keep the odor out, watching as Mr. Turrentine stepped into a closet and then back out with a bucket full of scrub brushes of various colors.

Turrentine moved down the line, handing each student in turn a scrub brush and a map. When he reached Colin, only a musty blue brush remained. The undesirable color notwithstanding, Colin was expected to take what was offered, just like everyone else.

"This is blue," Colin said.

"Yes, Fischer." Mr. Turrentine nodded. "I know this."

He turned to address the others. "Today," he said, "we give back. We will clean every bathroom in this building. We will scrub every toilet, we will scour every sink, we will mop every floor until you would be happy to lick Jell-O pudding off the tile. We will not discriminate on the basis of age, gender, or socioeconomic status. Are we clear?"

Everyone in line nodded emphatically, especially the boy who smelled like feet.

"Then what are you waiting for? Move with a sense of urgency."

The detainees moved—all but Colin, who had been studying his map and realized the bathroom he was expected to clean was by the cafeteria. This was easily the most horrific facility in the entire school, and Colin's head had already been in one of those toilets. It wasn't a pleasant memory.

"Problem, Fischer?"

"Yes," Colin said. He held up his scrub brush. "I don't like the color blue."

The bathroom by the cafeteria was even dirtier than Colin remembered from the first day of school.

At least, it was that way before Colin began cleaning. He found that once he mastered his horror and revulsion, he had a real talent for scrubbing out even the most difficult of stains. It helped to think of it as a problem that needed to be solved, rather than dirt, grime, and unspeakable human detritus that had to be washed away by hand.

That night, Colin wrote:

> Being a janitor is difficult. I wonder if janitors clean up after themselves, or if they leave it for other janitors. Tomorrow, I will ask them.

He was working on scrubbing the last toilet in the last stall when he heard the bathroom door open behind him. At first, Colin thought to confront whomever had walked in and point out the yellow sandwich board that was supposed to warn people away during the cleaning process. Then he heard a familiar, but trembling voice and decided it would be best not to show himself. Instead, he quietly pulled the stall door shut, crouched on the newly clean toilet seat, and listened very carefully. He wished he had his Notebook.

". . . I just want it all to go away," Colin heard Eddie say. But Eddie wasn't alone.

Two sets of footfalls clopped against the spotless tile floor as the door swung shut, leaving Eddie and his companion in apparent solitude. Colin could just make them out through the crack in the door. Eddie stood in front of the sink, and behind him—

"Pull yourself together," Rudy said. "You didn't even like the girl."

"That's not true. I love her."

"You love her. You love her so much, you let her swing while you walk around a free man. Excuse me while I dry a tear for the overwhelming humanity of it all. But your self-delusion and hypocrisy aren't at issue here."

Rudy leaned in close to Eddie, uncomfortably so. Colin realized his stall was visible in the mirror and hoped against hope that he would not be seen. He had only the scrub brush to defend himself.

Eddie slumped, bracing himself against the porcelain. "So can you help her or not?" he asked.

"My father is a partner at the most powerful law firm in Los Angeles. Of course I can help her." Rudy's eyes drifted across the mirror, toward Colin's stall. It was like Rudy knew Colin was there, though Colin calculated from the angle this was impossible.

Colin's heart slammed against his rib cage. A scream tickled his throat, demanding release. His legs and arms struggled to move—to cover his ears, to flee—but they could not. They were bound in place by force of will. Colin knew he could not be seen by Rudy, knew somehow this was important above all other things. Colin squeezed his eyes shut, a compromise with the instinct that battled his reason for supremacy.

Eddie nodded slowly. "Thanks, I guess."

Rudy patted Eddie on the back, but there was no comfort in it. He started to leave, but stopped, as he had one final message to deliver. "Eddie? Next time, put the gun in the right locker before your girlfriend finds it and decides to do you a favor. Your laziness cost me three hundred dollars. You're going to have to work that off."

"Yeah, okay," Eddie said. He sounded old, somehow. "How?"

Colin opened his eyes. He had to see. He wanted to

read the emotion on Rudy's face when he spoke next. He had to know what Rudy was, underneath.

Rudy smiled, but not with his eyes, like a shark considering a wounded seal. There was no emotion. There was nothing for Colin to read. There was nothing at all.

"Oh," Rudy sang, "I'm just full of great ideas." And then he was gone.

Colin watched Eddie, waiting for him to follow Rudy so he could escape his toilet prison and report back to Mr. Turrentine. But Eddie didn't leave. Instead, he entered the stall next to Colin and slammed the door closed. He didn't do any of the usual things Colin associated with someone going to the bathroom; Eddie simply sat down.

And Eddie wept.

Moments later, Colin burst out of the bathroom, clutching his scrub brush. He ran straight into Mr. Turrentine, who said nothing. He just looked at Colin, expecting some sort of report on the status of the task, but Colin was at a loss. They could hear the soft, muted sound of Eddie's sobs coming from inside the bathroom.

"Fischer. Is there something you want to tell me?"

"Yes," Colin said. He looked back at the bathroom, noting the yellow sandwich board. It was a warm color, much better than the scrub brush. "Do not go in there. Eddie needs privacy."

Mr. Turrentine nodded, thinking he understood. Perhaps he did.

"Can I go?" Colin asked.

"I don't know, can you go?"

It took Colin a moment to realize the question was rhetorical. Then he returned to the gym, grabbed his backpack and his Notebook, and ran home as fast he could. As he ran, he scribbled furiously in green ink, over and over again:

> . . . Moore, R.T. Moore, R.T. Moore, R.T. Moore, R.T. Moore, R.T. Moore, R.T. Moore, R.T. . . .

By the time he stopped, safe on his trampoline, Colin had filled an entire page.

The meticulously folded-up note Rudy found in his locker the next day was addressed to Moore, R.T. It read as follows:

> Football field. Today, 4:30 P.M. Come alone. —C.

And so Rudy found himself on the empty football field later that afternoon as asked. He was alone, as asked. He looked around himself, taking it all in. The field seemed so small when watching a game, but so large when standing in the center of it. Especially when you appeared to be the only person in the world.

It felt good to think so, and Rudy smiled. But only with his mouth.

"You."

The voice behind Rudy was not Colin Fischer's, nor did it seem the sort of thing that freak would say to begin a conversation. Rudy didn't have to turn around to know who had addressed him. What he did not know—what he found *fascinating*—was why.

"Wayne," Rudy said. "Wayne Connelly. Thus the 'C.'"

"Yeah," Wayne said. "Did I fool you?"

Rudy shrugged. The two boys walked toward each other. Each unafraid, each for different reasons. "It wasn't his handwriting," Rudy said. "It wasn't his style."

"He's a weird kid," Wayne allowed. "The truth is, I don't really have him figured out yet. But you? You I have all figured out."

"Oh, I can't wait."

"Colin solved the whole thing because he's really smart. He's not so good with people, but he was good enough to put together why Sandy had the gun in her purse and why Eddie had it in his locker. He even knew Eddie wasn't capable of making contact with *La Familia* and buying a gun on his own—he knew Eddie needed help. There was just one thing that didn't make any sense to him . . . but it makes sense to me."

Rudy considered Wayne for a long moment, noting everything about him. His clothes. Hairstyle. Shoes.

Everything, down to the dirt under his fingernails. Rudy committed every detail to memory with perfect recall. "And what's that?" Rudy asked.

"Why you helped him. How you had skin in the game. He asked me if I had ever done anything to you, if I had ever crossed you or one of the people you call your friends. I told him no. I told him in eight years, I had barely spoken to you."

"Then why did I do it?"

"Because you could," Wayne said. "Because you wanted to see what would happen next. You wanted to push a button and blow up somebody's world, whether it made any sense or not."

Rudy feigned horror. "That doesn't sound very nice at all."

"Here's the thing, dude. I know you're smart. You may be as smart as Colin. For all I know, you may be smarter. I don't care." Wayne moved up next to Rudy, chest to chest, staring down at him, blotting out the sun. "I don't give a damn how smart you are. If you ever do anything like this again—to *anyone*—I'll beat you stupid."

Wayne didn't wait for a reply. He turned on his heel and marched away. His business with Rudy was done, at least for today.

"Connelly," Rudy called after him. "I know you. I know where you went the first day of school, third period. I know what you do *after* school. I know everything."

"Then you know I'm serious," Wayne said, and he did not look back.

Moments later, Rudy was alone in the world once more. As he preferred.

EPILOGUE:
HUMAN BEHAVIOR

The word "altruism" dates only to the nineteenth century, but the mystery of why people are so willing to put the welfare of others before their own has consumed philosophers, theologians, and scientists for over two thousand years. If nature is a constant struggle between organisms for survival and sustenance, why would one creature ever sacrifice its own well-being in favor of another?

Religious texts tend to celebrate altruism and self-sacrifice, but often without explaining why it's preferable to love one's neighbor as oneself. The prospect of reward in the afterlife is sometimes dangled as payment for compassion and self-sacrifice, and that is that. But I find the idea of a heavenly quid pro quo distasteful and unsatisfactory.

Psychologists trace the origins of altruism to the emotion of empathy—the ability to feel the pain of another being as if experiencing it oneself. I don't like this explanation either. If the empathy-altruism hypothesis is correct, then a person is helping another to make his or her own suffering cease, making altruism just another form of selfishness.

Biologists, meanwhile, have invoked evolution in attempting to explain altruism, specifically the idea of kin selection. The theory goes that for most of history, humans lived together in small, closely related bands. When one hunter-gatherer helped another, he was actually helping ensure the survival of his own genes by proxy. Evolutionary mathematician JBS Haldane expressed the principle best when he declared, "I would lay down my life for two brothers or eight cousins." I find this explanation unsatisfactory, too. I only have one brother, but I would lay down my life for him if necessary.

I expressed this to Danny on his eleventh birthday, just before he blew out the candles and made his wish. He told me not to get his hopes up.

Colin bounced high in the air—higher, perhaps, than he had ever bounced before, pushing the elasticity of the trampoline to its limits. The springs pulled the fabric taut, groaning with the strain, but held as Colin landed and soared once more into the clear, blue San Fernando Valley sky.

Wayne stood at the foot of the trampoline with a DUBIOUS frown, arms crossed.

"No, really!" Colin exclaimed as his feet floated above Wayne's head. "It helps you think!" he shouted as he belly-flopped onto the fabric and rebounded. "And now it's an Olympic sport!"[35] He tucked into a forward flip and performed it expertly.

Colin's enthusiasm was difficult to dismiss. It was even more difficult to dismiss when Colin slowed to a light hop and beckoned Wayne onto the trampoline, insistent but unassuming. "Try it."

"What the hell," Wayne said. He shrugged, addressed the aluminum frame, and unsteadily pulled himself over the pad and onto the mat with no small sense of CONCERN.

Colin reached out to help.

Wayne's outstretched hand froze an inch from Colin's, suddenly uncertain. He'd never seen Colin touch anyone on purpose, and the consequences of unwanted physical contact were well documented.

---

35 Trampoline has been an official, competitive Olympic sport in the gymnastics category since the 2000 games in Sydney, Australia. The highest recorded score is still held by the first male gold medalist, Alexandre Moskalenko of Russia, who was awarded a rating of 41.7.

Wayne looked in Colin's eyes, searching for an answer he knew would not be written there.

Colin splayed his fingers, reaching further.

Now, Wayne understood. He accepted Colin's offer, long enough to stand. The trampoline wobbled, punishing his inexperience, but Colin would not let him fall. He was stronger than Wayne imagined.

Then, his confidence growing, Wayne let go of Colin's hand. He bounced. A test flight, and a successful one. Wayne bounced higher, and grinned. Colin grinned too. He was not mirroring Wayne, and he was not following a script. He felt JOY.

Colin's parents stood together at the kitchen window. They watched in silence, struck by the effortlessness of their son's play and the ease of his connection to Wayne. The sight was unprecedented.

Mrs. Fischer smiled. "He's really gonna be okay, isn't he?"

Mr. Fischer smiled back and pulled his wife close to him, his eyes locked on his boy with his new friend. Possibly from the look of things, the best friend Colin had ever had. Then Mr. Fischer frowned. He knew he should be happy, but somehow . . . he saw his own face reflected in the glass and wondered what Colin would make of him now.

"Life is a mystery," he said.

Outside, Colin was too busy making plans to notice his father's expression. If he had, he would not have understood why his father looked SAD. It was not a thing for boys to understand until they became fathers themselves, and this strange moment arrived.

"We could train together," Colin declared breathlessly. "Compete in the pairs category . . ." Colin laid out his Olympic vision, and Wayne listened, and they bounced into the late summer sky together.

Each in their own way, they knew Rudolph Talbott Moore was far from finished with them. He had declared war, and there would be consequences. Colin and Wayne did not speak of it. For now, the future was a trampoline.

For now, they were just boys. And what could be better than that?

The End

ACKNOWLEDGMENTS

Victory may have a thousand fathers, but thanking every-one who made *Colin Fischer* possible would require bloating this little book to doorstop proportions. Nevertheless, attention must be paid. So a heartfelt thank you to . . .

. . . Our wonderful lit agent Eric Simonoff for encouraging us to finish this book, then going out and selling it.

. . . Our editors Ben Schrank and Gillian Levinson, who have been wonderful collaborators and infinitely patient in teaching neophyte novelists the ins and outs of the book world.

. . . Multi-hyphenate genius and friend Lev Grossman for his encouragement and support.

. . . Shawna Benson, who can probably recite this book from memory and knows every comma intimately.

. . . Our film and TV agents, managers, and attorneys, who have been tireless in advocating and protecting the book (and us) through this entire process. So thank you also to Paul Haas, Jeff Gorin and the whole team at WME (Kimberly, Tom, Zach, and Jordan), Allen Fischer at PYE, and Ken Richman and Gretchen Bruggeman-Rush at HJTH.

Finally, a special thank you to Susan Solomon, our Mama Bear. Without her, the sun doesn't rise and the world doesn't turn.

Susan, we're sorry your favorite word isn't in this book.

ABOUT THE AUTHORS

ASHLEY EDWARD MILLER and ZACK STENTZ met on the Internet, a consequence of their mutual love of all things *Star Trek*. Together, Miller and Stentz have written and/or produced over a hundred hours of television. Most recently, they co-wrote the films *X-Men: First Class* and *Thor*. Upcoming projects include *The Fall Guy* and a *Starship Troopers* remake. Miller and Stentz both live in Los Angeles. Find out more at: facebook.com/colinfischerbook.

ADMIRING

 EXCITED

 AMUSED

 JEALOUS

 BASHFUL

 EMBARRASSED

 WARM

 CRUEL

 DISGUSTED

 HOPEFUL

 ASTONISHED

 EXASPERATED

 HAPPY

 HESITANT

 CERTAIN

 SERIOUS

 WARY

 HOSTILE

 DUBIOUS

 INDIFFERENT

 SHOCKED

 SHY

 INTERESTED

 SUSPICIOUS